the devil stood up

A Novel by Christine Dougherty
www.christinedoughertybooks.com

To Peter Conradi
Best Regards!
Christine Dougherty

The Devil Stood Up

Also by Christine Dougherty:

Faith, Creation
Faith was three the first time her twin sister died.
The second time, she was ten. Discover the paradox of
Faith. Book One in the Faith Series.

Messages
James Smith is receiving messages. Will he find the
right answers? Follow James as he pieces together the
puzzle in this taut, psychological thriller. You'll be
guessing until the last page.

Darkness Within, A Collection of Horrorific Short Stories
These bone-chilling, mind-wrenching short stories
will leave you wondering about the people around
you…and yourself.

Special thanks to the early readers. Your help is profoundly important and the book is better for having been in your hands:
Chrissy, James, Ann, Anthony, and Pauline

* * *

And to my number one fan, my husband Steve Dougherty who is steadfast, tireless, and patient in his support:
Love you, Biggie

BOOK ONE

The Devil Slept

The Devil rolled over, swiping a knotted forearm across his dripping brow. Half asleep, struggling, uncomfortable, The Litany of the evils of the world slipped through his unconsciousness like fine wisps of acrid smoke, intertwining, interweaving, noxious, and necessary.

This is how he thought of the million threads of evil that bound his mind, they were: The Litany.

The evil of the world spiked sharply, spoiling his sleep, but he could not stop it any more than he could have stopped time or stopped the evil itself. He rolled, almost coming awake, flirting with full consciousness, and then settled as the streaming evil flatlined, becoming bearable again.

This body, even, was uncomfortable: difficult to position with grace and never entirely at rest, not really. He'd never gotten used to it, never become accustomed to losing grace. The weight, the stink and yes, even the sight of it was unbearable, because in Heaven, there'd been no ugliness, no stink, no uncomfortable body, only awareness and beauty.

The Devil had never been a human, but knew them well enough by now to think that this must be what it felt like, to be in a body. Heavy. Tethered. Stinking. And the Devil didn't have a mere human body—what he had was much, much worse. Hulking, with bony extrusions on his forehead, back of his neck, knuckles, elbows and ankles. Muscles that seemed to work at cross-purposes, snarling into knots and pulling his arms down even as he struggled to lift them, causing a constant, grinding pain along the bone. Joints that screamed of impossibly tight tendons. Feet so humped and bumped they resembled large hooves. And over all this terrible hulk of a body, blackish blood streamed continuously, never staunched, leaving bloody trails and pools wherever he went.

The Devil ran an arm over his forehead again, sliding it through the viscous and salty combination of blood and sweat on his brow. The dailyness of human evil flowed through and through him, waxing and waning.

He saw himself through the eyes of the humans who ended up with him—the nightmare visage he was. The ones he, the Devil, was bound by God, Himself to punish. And he saw something else in them, the evil humans—the petty, the weak, the greedy, the mean-hearted—he saw that they held him, the Devil, accountable.

They all blamed him, unable to bear the weight of their own sins, of their own choices. They stared at him in abject terror and the Devil felt it in their tiny, limited, misguided minds again and again, one common, jittery thought: the Devil made me do it. Then the Devil would roll his figurative sleeves and turn to the work of punishment.

For punishment was his only purpose.

And the punishment was simple: they burned, and they burned, and they burned.

And they would continue to burn until God, Himself decided that it was enough. Then, and only then, they would cease to exist on any plane, putting an end to their torment.

The Devil stoked the fires of their burning with his ferocious dragon's breath, blood and sweat pouring from him endlessly, his acrid blood itself an incendiary agent, like gasoline.

He punished one no harder than the others. His place was not that of judgment. Only to punish, and punish, and punish, until God, Himself saw fit to take this job from him and lift him back, weightless, body-less to heaven and to grace.

Or to snap him, too, out of existence.

Sometimes this weighed heavily on his mind, this thought of non-existence. He knew that if he did not exist he wouldn't care–he wouldn't be around to care. But he also chafed at the thought of non-existence. He butted up against it most often in his sleep, his thoughts turning resentful under the heinous weight of The Litany as it ran non-stop through his mind.

He knew every evil that existed, every evil that put humans in his grasp, and yet considered his punishment the worst of all, and for what was he being punished?

That he, the Anointed One, beautiful Angel Lucifer, had considered himself better than God, Himself.

And was his punishment just?

If God, Himself said it was so…then it was.

* * *

The Devil rolled again, uneasy, The Litany waxing as Free Will ran rampant through weak hearts and weak minds on Earth.

Bit by bit, he became aware of the musings of a woman-child sparking like cold, reddish-purple electrical fire along the line of The Litany. He didn't often catch individual evils and hadn't for millennia. They were too layered, too intertwined, but this was different, the way it tugged and snagged along the current of The Litany like a lure and line encrusted log bobbing noxiously. She: resentful of the boy-child she'd given birth to. She'd been seventeen when she got pregnant and her parents had been mad and she hadn't cared about them being mad, and then her parents had accepted it but then her mother had tortured her with a constant stream of:

"Carrie, you need to stop drinking, it'll hurt the baby."

And: "Carrie, you'll have to stay home once the baby gets here, it'll need all your attention, sweetheart."

And: "Your Daddy and I want you to finish high school, so, I'll watch the baby for you during the day, but maybe you could get some part time work on the weekends to help us out." She just went and on and on and more and more until Carrie felt as though she'd like to stab her mother in the throat just to get her to shut the hell up about it.

She had no intention of finishing high school; she already felt as though she'd just been marking time there even before she got pregnant. School held nothing for her, the teachers were all assholes and jerks, most of the other students were assholes and jerks, the classes were boring beyond belief. They never talked about anything she wanted to talk about, which was mainly herself. And she couldn't figure that out. Personally, she thought she was way more fascinating than those dumbass kids they showed on MTV. They should do a reality show about her. About how awesome her life was. Or at least, how awesome it was going to be once she was eighteen and could finally do whatever the hell she wanted to do.

But in the meantime, the pregnancy brought her a satisfying amount of attention. The school had wanted to kick her out, but everyone had told her she should fight for her rights! They had no cause to kick her out! And they were damn right, too, Carrie thought, and she envisioned how she would fight the school and they would put her story all over the internet and she would become a celebrity! But then she couldn't get it figured out, how to fight the school, and no one else seemed to know what she should be doing, just that she should fight. That didn't do her any damn good, so the whole thing went by the wayside and she quit school even before her junior year ended.

Dropping out was okay with her, because by that time, she was showing, really showing, and people paid all sorts of attention to her. They gave up their seats on the bus and everyone was always offering her treats, and smiling at her like she was a superstar or something. Even her friends were treating her better although she got the impression that a couple of them were talking behind her back and calling her a loser for getting pregnant and for not saying who the dad was. She knew that one of them had posted something along those lines on Facebook, but had deleted her as a friend so Carrie didn't see it herself—only heard about it from someone else.

She'd acted really mysterious about the dad, tried to make out like she couldn't say…like he was a mafia guy or a married guy or maybe even a famous dude. But the truth was, she didn't know who the father was. Well, she knew who it was but not his name or where he was from or anything. He was just a random guy she'd done it with at a concert. She'd made him buy her a t-shirt and a beer and then she'd fucked him behind the port-a-potties.

She liked making guys do things for her. Most of them would do something, buy her a present or take her somewhere to eat—somewhere fancy like Red Lobster or Outback. The fancy restaurants were the best, but she'd settle for anything, really, as long as the guy bought and told her she was so pretty, so awesome. She'd been having sex since she was fourteen and had known that she could get pregnant…she'd always just figured she wouldn't because she didn't want to.

Then there was the baby shower and though it wasn't anything like the Super Sweet Sixteen parties on MTV, it was still okay. Nice to be the center of attention and to get presents. She'd been so excited by the stack of them on the sideboard in her Mother's dining room, but then, when they sat her in the chair with the fancy umbrella and she'd started opening the presents, everything had been for the baby. There were no presents for her. No iPod, no clothes, no gift cards…what the fuck? Her mood had shifted and when Mrs. Allen, their seventy year old neighbor, had tried to rub her belly murmuring "oooohh, what a sweet little—" Carrie had slapped her hand away and sneered nastily:

"Christ! Lay off me, okay, you fucking child molester? Stop fucking rubbing me. It's fucking gross."

And Mrs. Allen had backed off, mouth agape, face turning bright, bright red. Mean satisfaction flowed through Carrie, soothing her nerves.

Dumb old cunt, she thought, she has no right to paw me like that. Fucking trying to cop a feel.

Her mother had come to Mrs. Allen and cupped her by the elbow and Carrie heard whispered snatches of her mother's conversation: "…so sorry, she just hasn't been feeling…" and "…can I get you a piece of cake to…" and "…if you're sure, but it's not over until three and you're more than welcome to…" but Mrs. Allen was already at the door, shaking her head, her smile a tight, polite line bisecting the middle of her face. She glanced back at Carrie and Carrie raised her eyebrows at her like yeah, so? And smirked again. Mrs. Allen dropped her eyes. Probably she wouldn't come around again and Carrie saw the sadness on her mom's face–Mrs. Allen was a good friend to her–and Carrie felt that soothing wash of cold satisfaction once more.

But all in all, the shower had been good, for the attention. Everyone watching everything she did, listening to everything she said and falling all over themselves to laugh at her jokes. That felt…right. Like the way it should be.

Then the doctors appointments, with the nurses giving her cookies and juice because they said she was too thin! Honey you need to gain weight for your baby! But Carrie was careful not to gain too much weight. The baby could come out skinny for all she cared as long as it meant she wouldn't look like a cow once she got it out of her. Plus, a skinny baby was better than a fat one, because she for sure didn't want a fat kid.

But then going to the hospital had been a fucking horror show. Giving birth to it had been the worst thing in the world. At first, she'd been able to pretend like she was in a movie: a brave young woman giving birth and all eyes were on her as she suffered in silence and everyone in the hospital would be talking about the amazing girl who'd been so brave, braver than anyone had ever been before! But in reality, it had hurt so fucking much and they told her they couldn't give her anything because the baby was in distress, and she'd yelled:

"In distress? Are you fucking kidding me? Who gives a shit about that fucker? I am in fucking distress! My fucking cunt is ripping open! Now give me something you bunch of fucking assholes!"

The nurses had silenced, cutting their eyes to Carrie's mother who stood next to Carrie, tears streaming down her face. Carrie's mother wouldn't meet the eyes of the nurses. Couldn't. She shook as she felt the rage coming off her daughter in waves, almost real enough to ripple the air above her and she remembered Carrie even as an infant consumed by this same rage. Her tiny body a stiffening board; head, shoulders and heels the only things touching the blanket in her crib as she bowed up tensely, red-faced and raging.

Afterwards, they'd brought Carrie the thing in a blanket. The nurse had stood next to the bed and pulled back the corner of the baby's blanket, her face open and expectant, excited to share the joy a young mother felt at the sight of her first born.

Carrie looked.

It was red faced, ugly, its head smooshed on one side, white hair covering its forehead and shoulders, a blister on its puckered asshole of a mouth, tiny veins visible under its thin, pale skin and Carrie had been horrified.

"Ugh, what's wrong with it? Get it away from me!"

The nurse had drawn back sharply, but Carrie's mother stepped forward, smiling, and the nurse handed the baby over. Carrie's mother looked down into the little face so much like Carrie's had been but full of such a deep peacefulness that Carrie's mom forgot for a moment where she was and who she was, as she fell in love with her grandson.

"Ma. What's wrong with it? You can tell me; I can take it," Carrie said, straightening her shoulders and glancing after the retreating nurse, hoping the nurse had heard what she'd said. Heard how brave she'd been and would tell everyone.

"There's nothing wrong with him, sweetheart. He's perfect," she said and brought the baby back to Carrie. She hesitated for a second before she put the baby in Carrie's arms—some red flash of caution zoomed across her mind and then was gone.

Carrie's face shriveled in disgust at what lay in her arms and she shook her head.

"Huh-uh, this does not look right. It doesn't look like a baby. It's sick or something. I know it is," she said.

"Sweetheart, that's what babies look like when they're newborns. You're thinking of a six-month baby all filled out and active. He'll get there; I promise!"

Carrie's mother smiled at her, but Carrie didn't look up to see it. She stared into the baby's face. Even its eyelids, she saw, were tissue-paper thin. It took a hitching breath and opened its mouth in a gummy yawn. It looked so vulnerable. Then it opened its deep, slate eyes and stared up at Carrie and she felt something shift deep inside herself, and realized that she was more than disgusted by this warm, quiescent bundle her mother had put in her arms, she was furious with it. She wanted to shake it and throw it down on the ground. But she knew that wasn't allowed. Hurriedly, she shoved it back to her mother.

"Here, take it back. I don't want to look at it." She'd rolled over and pulled the thin hospital blanket up over her shoulder and closed her eyes. "Tell them to hurry up getting my damn room ready." She felt better immediately.

But then the nurses had come in and tried to make her feed it; her mother pushed for this, too, wanting her to whip out her tit in front of everyone and let the little monster latch on. It made her feel sick to her stomach that something was leeching off of her that way. Plus, that's what the boys she slept with always wanted to do, suck on her, and it was gross that this thing did the same…like it was born a pig.

So she was just as glad when the monster turned its face away from her, mewling piggishly and clenching its little pig hands. Then they let her pump and she was glad because she could do that in private, plus this way she'd still get the fast weight loss like she'd read about in People magazine. How all the stars with babies got super-slimmed down super-quick by sucking themselves dry.

When she got home, it was a little bit better. She had her own television again and was excited because the DVR had filled up with her shows from the last two days. But every time she tried to watch something, someone came over wanting to see the monster. Especially after she'd taken a picture of her and the monster and made sure she was smiling and posted it as her Facebook status and wrote:

"Brian is fiiinnnnallly heeeeeeer! So so so happy n he is the BEST n sweetst baby! Soooooo happy 2 have my little 'Bri-Bri'!"

So many people posted on her wall and sent messages. It was really great.

She told her mother to take a picture of her kissing the monster and she posted that one on Facebook and everyone was saying "aaaaawwwwww!" and "bless you both!" and "so happy 4 u he is adorbz!"

She spent hours reading the messages and sending messages back and the monster cried and cried until finally she'd gone into her parents' room and yelled at it to quit it. And then, of course, her mother had come in with all her "honey, he's just a baby" nonsense. As if she didn't realize the pig baby was really just a giant pain in the ass.

It took three years of being stuck with it–being told what to do with it, how to raise it, how to talk to it, how not to talk to it, how to dress and feed it–for her to finally get fed up. The pregnancy had been cool because she got the attention, but now everyone paid attention to the monster. Nobody even hardly acknowledged her birthday, but when the monster had one, they broke the bank to celebrate. It really got on her nerves. It was like she didn't exist anymore. She was just the monster's mother.

So, she decided to get rid of it.

* * *

How much time passes on Earth while the Devil sleeps? Is it days or years? Is it relative?

The Litany, bit and chopped at by the musings of the woman-child that wanted to kill her own son kept on and on, the low undercurrent so much like an adjunct to the Devil's own thoughts that they may as well have been.

The Devil rolled on his bunk, his bony extrusions scraping across his rocky bed of the damned and he waved one dripping fist, thrusting it out as if to push something away, his breath rushing out and igniting the blood that had puddled around him, almost waking, then fading back, falling back into The Litany as the story of Carrie Walsh continued to flow.

* * *

She wasn't sure how to go about getting rid of it, but she was sure that today was the day because her dad was at work and her mother was at an all-day charity event with the other hospice workers where she volunteered.

She'd just have to figure it out as she went along. How hard could it be to kill one little kid?

She'd dressed it in its favorite blue shorts from Nana and favorite t-shirt with the sailboat appliquéd on the front and pressed its feet–sticky like gross little sticky buns–into the baby sandals. She'd brushed its blond, duck-fluff hair while it smiled at her, toothy and toothless, blue eyed and grinning.

She'd looked in the medicine cabinet in her parent's bedroom and considered the things she found there. Razors. Pills. Peroxide. Iodine. Would iodine kill the kid? She stood looking at the bottle, considering. Worth a shot. Might only make him sick, but, whatever.

"Brian!" she said, "I have something for you!" She sing-songed her voice the way she knew he liked. The way her mother did it. Lilting and fake. Carrie knew it must be fake when her mother did it, because it felt fake when Carrie did it.

"Bri-Bri, I have a nice surprise-prise!"

He tottered in, tiny toes gripping the front edges of his sandals, his hands going to the appliquéd boat for reassurance, caressing nervously. He was afraid of his mama when they were alone in the house. He preferred nana and pop-pop to be around. He preferred his nana and pop-pop.

"Mama's gonna give you something yummy, Bri-Bri, you want something yummy in your tummy?" She bent over him, vulturous, a wide smile that showed even her back teeth.

Brian nodded uncertainly, trying to smile back but nervous. He loved his Mama with all his heart, but never really knew what to expect from her. Never knew which Mama would appear.

Carrie imitated her mother, the way her mother had been when the monster had gone through that gross picky stage where it only ate half of what they tried to give it. Food all over its face, neck, hands, chair—revolting.

"Open wide and close your eyes and you will get a big surprise," she said, advancing on him, unscrewing the cap from the iodine bottle.

Brian recognized the charm his nana had used and

knew it meant good things were coming and he relaxed. He closed his eyes and tilted his head back, opening his mouth. The golden duck fluff bobbed on his cowlick and he looked for all the world like a hungry baby bird. Carrie's features twisted in disgust and she tilted the bottle into his pink mouth. It splashed cold and brownish-red over his tongue and she caught a whiff of the iodine–a smell like thin, tinny blood.

Brian swallowed once, reflexively, and twisted his head aside, one hand coming up sharply, connecting with the iodine bottle. Carrie dropped it and it splashed across the bathroom floor, bloodying the rug and walls.

"Goddammit!" she said. "You little fuck look what you did!"

She drew back her hand to strike the monster but he'd bent double, gagging and crying. Her stomach lifted and dropped, a fun roller coaster feeling–it's dying, it's dying, her mind shouted exultantly. If I knew it would have been this easy, I would have–but then he heaved and threw up the iodine.

Then he heaved again.

And again.

Carrie looked at the bottle on the floor, the mess on the walls and rug, the biley red vomit the monster had produced. She looked at Brian, lying on his side, screaming, crying, his face red as his chest hitched and hitched again. Then he was beyond making sound, his mouth a ragged red 'o' of fear and pain and he couldn't get his breath at all. A bright spark flickered in her mind again— maybe this is it–but she wasn't as excited this time and with good reason because look, it pulled in a breath and then continued to cry.

Shit.

Now what?

Now she'd have to clean up, that was fucking what. Why did nothing ever go right for her?

She stripped Brian and set him in the dry tub.

"Sit there," she said. "Don't move."

He sat, muzzy and sick, disoriented.

She cleaned the bathroom, scrubbing at the walls until there were only faint pink rows of dots and dashes to show where the iodine had splashed. She took the rug and threw it in the washer, dumped bleach and soap on top of it and set it to hot. If it didn't clean up, she'd just toss it. Her mother could get another cheap Wal-Mart bathmat.

She scrubbed the tile, her back to the tub. Brian curled over onto his side, shivering, a thin trickle of iodine and drool descending from the corner of his mouth. She forgot he was there as she scrubbed and her thoughts turned to her unluckiness, how hard everything was for her. She thought her life would have really started by now. She thought she'd be somebody. Now she couldn't even get a guy cause she'd have to tell them about the monster and then they wouldn't want anything to do with her anymore no matter how much she had sex with them. She was getting so old, almost twenty-one. She was wasting herself.

Brian whimpered from the tub and Carrie turned.

"Okay, Shitheap, let's get new clothes on you. Christ, you made a mess," she lifted him by one arm until he struggled to get his feet under him on the slippery enamel of the tub. "You fucked up your favorite shirt. Nana's gonna hate your guts for that."

Brian looked up groggily at the mention of Nana. He wanted his nana so badly right now. He really wanted her and pop-pop. He wished they would come home. His feet slipped out from under him. His logy thoughts were knocked askew by a new blast of pain, fresh and blinding, originating in his shoulder and spreading up his arm and over his chest and back.

Carrie had dislocated his shoulder.

His scream was rough, grinding over his chemical-burned vocal cords. Carrie shook him furiously and he screamed again and something gave way in his throat and then he was choking, choking on a trickle of hot blood.

"Jesus! Just shut up! What the hell is wrong with you?" She shook him again and then noticed the way his shoulder seemed to have grown oddly humped, and how he twisted on his arm, the shoulder blade pinned back at an unnatural angle.

"Oh Christ, you dislocated your shoulder again," she said. A small trill of fear went though her. He'd done this once before, when he'd been around two. He'd dislocated his shoulder while her mother had been out shopping and her father was watching a ballgame in the back den. They'd given her holy hell for that one, too. She couldn't let them see this. It didn't occur to her that her parents wouldn't care about a dislocated shoulder if Brian were dead. But Carrie couldn't really think more than five seconds ahead.

"Brian, lay down," she said, her voice calm and stern and it cut through the hot fog of his pain and he collapsed onto the cold bathroom tiles and pressed his cheek to the numbing coolness. Carrie took his chubby baby arm in both her hands and tried to force his arm down, not really sure how to make it go like they'd done in the hospital. They'd knocked Brian out first and then twisted it somehow and it had kind of snapped back into place.

She twisted as she pushed and the monster's screams rose in pitch beyond her ability to hear and then the monster's screams stopped all at once. He had fainted. She twisted his arm this way and that and pushed and pushed—it was a lot easier without all the screaming—

but she still couldn't make it go back in.

Fuck.

Now what?

* * *

While the monster slept, she put fresh clothes on it. The yellow shorts went on easily enough, but the t-shirt was going to be impossible with his shoulder all cock-eyed. She found a little tank top with shoulder snaps instead, blue with a friendly green dragon. The dragon was cute. She smiled as she looked at it.

She looked down at the monster. Its hair was stained pinkish red on one side and a scabby looking line of bloodied vomit had dried across its cheek. Its arm jutted oddly. Its belly swelled against the elastic band of its shorts.

It stank.

Carrie knew this thing had come from her, she knew it was a thing that would eventually grow up to be a person, but it wasn't really a person yet, was it? No. Not really. Although sometimes, when it was babbling to nana or pop-pop, its little voice peeping, she'd felt a small twist of something…jealousy maybe or curiosity? She wasn't sure. She'd look at its bright little blue eyes and turned up nose and think that it was pretty cute, getting cuter all the time, actually.

But still.

It was also a giant pain in the ass.

She yanked the tank top down over its head, struggling it over its belly and snapping the catches at the shoulders. She went back to the bathroom and wet a cloth and scrubbed the line of vomit from its face.

Christ it looks like it's been in a car accident, she thought.

A car accident.

An idea formed in her mind: a tragic accident, her picture in the paper, a hot newsguy coming out to interview her, riding in a limo at the funeral…everyone's attention on her as she…what was the word? As she grieved. She could put it on Facebook too. Probably she'd have even more people flocking to her page.

Because her baby got run over by the car. She'd seen it on the news before; it happened all the time. Kids were always getting killed by their own mother's minivans and that's what the stories always said—tragic. It would explain the dislocated shoulder, too, and her parents wouldn't be able to get mad at her for it.

Yes, so tragic.

A tragic accident.

She popped the front door open and looked out, checking both ways, making sure none of the neighbors were out. It was hot this late in the morning. The hottest day so far this summer. And humid. Her hair was going to be a mess, but she'd just have to try and get a brush through it before the first news vans showed up.

Brian struggled and moaned foggily as if caught in a bad dream.

"Shhhh, baby," she said, her voice soft. She didn't look down at the rag-tag bundle in her arms. "Gonna be okay, baby."

He moaned again and she checked left and right once more and then stepped out onto the porch. There was a good screen of trees and bushes between all the houses. As long as no one came out, she'd be all right.

She trotted to her car–a Dodge Stratus her parents had bought for her and that she nastily referred to as a Dodge Lack-of-Status–and lay Brian in front of it, on the black-top between the car and the garage. She stepped back and tilted her head. Hmm. That might not work. It just looked–wrong somehow. How about if she…

Brian struggled and his eyes cracked open; two wet slits in his face.

"Mama mama," he said, his voice fractured and whis-pery.

The pain was still immense, but now the nausea was starting to overtake it. He felt the fire of the blacktop baking into his shoulders and legs and he tried to right himself, struggling to keep his dislocated shoulder still. Vertigo sent the world reeling up and over him. His mama was dragging something, his Big Wheel, taking it past him, the plastic wheels gritting sharply on the driveway.

"Mama mama," he said again, whispering, not wanting her to go away, beginning to cry and then her hand was on his face, cool and comforting. Caressing.

"Shhhh, baby, go to sleep. Just sleep Bri-Bri and mama is gonna get you all fixed up. Don't cry."

Then lifting him, lifting him away from the fire. And his arm was a sheet of agony but her taking the fire away was so good and then he felt cool, hard plastic at his back. He squinted his eyes open once more and the handles of the Big Wheel were before him, red and set at a jaunty angle, gold streamers flashing in the sun. But he didn't want to ride his Big Wheel. He wanted to lie in the bed. He wanted nana. He wanted pop-pop.

He put his good hand out and pushed the Big Wheel handle, trying to push himself up and out of the seat.

"Mama," he said and grunted with pain as the handles turned and he lost his grip and plopped back down on the plastic seat.

A roar filled his mind and at first he thought it was the pain from his shoulder or from his belly coming to get him, made alive with magic. His chin rested tiredly on his chest and when he opened his eyes the first thing he saw was the dragon on his tank top, green and grinning, upside down with a million teeth and it looked like it was getting bigger and bigger, blowing a hot, choking cloud over him and he coughed and the tear in his throat bled again and the dragon's eyes were huge and black and then filling with a bright burst of red fire, and his last confused thought before the bumper overtook him was:

The dragon is getting me...!

* * *

The Devil knew little of true grief in The Litany, only self-pity and vaulting self-worth. What little he could glimpse was through the damned, those already earmarked by God, Himself for punishment. The damned understood very little of true grief. They saw things only in terms of themselves, like infants grown obnoxious with too much age and size. They shit and shit and waited, legs akimbo, for the world to clean them up. And they did get cleaned up, eventually, but most likely not in the way they thought it would happen.

God, Himself decreed that they would be cleansed by fire.

The Devil rolled again, more blood coursing over the tortured contours of his body, dripping and puddling, burning, consuming over and over without destroying the legion of damned. He swam to brief consciousness, aware of The Litany and Carrie's miniscule part in it and wondered briefly why this crime–noxious as it was but still unoriginal, mundane, even–should catch his attention so, should disturb his sleep.

Carrie's contribution to The Litany held glimpses of the deep grief of her parents, as seen through Carrie's eyes, and she did not understand their grief. She saw it, and realized she was the cause of it, or, more to the point, the monster's death was the cause of it, but she was annoyed by her mother's near catatonia. Her father's withdrawal from the world.

It siphoned so much of the attention away from her.

* * *

She'd done everything right. Called 911, been hysterical, cried when the ambulance and police arrived. She had sobbed, but had been unable to produce tears, no matter how much she tried to think of upsetting things: getting acid in her face and becoming ugly, getting fat like her mother, getting wrinkly like her father. Nothing produced actual tears.

In the hospital, where they tried to untangle the monster's mangled body, her mother had come in and found

Carrie sitting in a corridor, picking at her nails, waiting for some doctor or other to come out. A police officer stood opposite, leaned against the corridor wall and watched as Carrie examined herself, a small moue of disgust crossing her features as she tried to dig the blood from under one perfectly shaped fingernail. The cop crossed his arms over his chest as a disturbing certainty whispered into his cop's mind.

Carrie's mother paused, the scene before her like a slap, realizing two things at once: the cop thought Carrie had something to do with Brian's death and so did she. In fact, she was sure of it. The realization took her heart and first squeezed it with merciless strength that took her breath away and then clad it, burning and smoking, in thick steel, making it impervious, shielding it for the days she saw were coming. She felt the extra weight in her heart just as surely as if there had been actual bands of hot metal binding it.

Through the funeral and then the rumors, the investigation and then the arrest, she'd kept her heart clad. She'd kept her doubts to herself. She'd helped her husband along and let her friends comfort her until the rumors became so rampant that even the best of her friends couldn't ignore them and then they, too, pulled away. Even that was a relief of sorts. A weight lifted.

Then the lawyer had appeared at the door.

Thomas Evigan was a good lawyer. He could have been great, but his intentions were not to be a great lawyer, his intentions were to be a great politician. Political office was his ultimate goal.

He'd defended legions of people, some innocent, most not, but had had very little true exposure as of yet. He watched the case of the girl who ran over her little boy with great interest. It remained somewhat local news, due to the fickle nature of news consumers, but he thought he could make it more than that. He looked into the soulless eyes of the pretty young mother when they flashed her booking photo and in those Gila orbs he saw something he recognized: he saw someone much like himself. With one of his most important attributes.

Misguidedly, Thomas Evigan thought of his self-centered narcissism as ambition.

He saw a matching ambition in the eyes of Carrie Walsh. And he thought, if she was game, then he might be able to get from this case what he'd been needing for some time: headlines. Publicity. People wouldn't care who he represented as long as he looked good while he was doing it.

He read about the case and mulled over the details. For the police, it was a slam-dunk. They had everything they needed to convict. They weren't even putting the big dogs on it, that's how confident they were. But the one thing they didn't have, the one thing that he could use, build upon, was that she had never confessed.

He'd found her parent's address and met with them.

Then he met with Carrie and devised THE STORY as he felt she should tell it.

It was at this point that he–unknowingly–joined The Litany.

Christine Dougherty

BOOK TWO

The Devil Woke Up

The spark of Thomas Evigan joined the spark of Carrie in The Litany and when they met, they flared so strongly that the Devil woke up.

After all the theft and lies, greed, murder, hate, all the cheating and using, the molestation, beating, and the killing, the torture and self pity, the Devil felt the musings of Thomas Evigan as he studied pictures of the little boy Brian alive and well and then studied pictures of the sad corpse in yellow terry shorts and friendly green dragon tank top and saw in them the code, the key, the path to his rise, his rise to fame, and the Devil rolled onto his side and sat up, groaning. The damned groaned beneath him like an echoing, sycophantic chorus.

Bent with the weight, the unbearable weight of The Litany, and this new thread which somehow weighted it to breaking, the Devil leaned his head into his aching, pulsing, bleeding hands. He felt the weight of The Litany as he'd never felt it before and it drove his head further into his hands and he rocked it—giant, misshapen monolith that it was. He rolled his head from side to side and leaned further forward, his great elbows grinding against his great knees and a slightly less viscous fluid flowed over his hands, thinning the blood and he leveled his hands before his eyes and saw what he'd never expected to see: tears.

He blinked his burning eyes and a fresh cascade of saline heartbreak washed over his face, hotter even than his flammable blood.

The Litany continued, Thomas Evigan meeting with Carrie, telling her The Story as he wanted her to tell it: that Carrie's father had poisoned the baby with iodine, that Carrie's mother had run the baby over, that Carrie, herself, had been horribly abused by both parents as she was growing up. Carrie told Thomas Evigan that she hadn't been abused at all, that in fact her parents were weak, weak pushovers. Thomas Evigan reiterated to Carrie that she had, indeed, been abused, that was why she'd appeared remorseless after her baby was killed. That was why she had lied to cover for them; she was afraid of them, in fact. Thomas Evigan could already see the dramatic headlines. He pictured this remorseless bitch on the stand, crying, grieving the loss of her own childhood and the loss of her beloved baby. It would be on the news every day. In the papers every day. On the internet every day. And along with it would be his name, his face, ubiquitous. He thrilled at the idea, his hands closing unconsciously on the pictures of the mangled baby Brian, crushing them in his closed fist. Crushing further the sad, badly used toddler's body taking up a mere third of the cold morgue table.

Carrie mulled it over, weighing her pride against being in jail. She hadn't minded jail so far, it was not that bad. There were many women in there for hurting or killing their own children or allowing them to be hurt or killed by family, boyfriends, friends. She balked at making it seem as though her parents had got the best of her. She wanted this lawyer to prove it was an accident, a horrible accident, so she could post more on her Facebook about how terrible the ordeal had been.

She'd posted from the hospital, the day Brian had…died…she'd posted: "2 sad 2 beleve my sweet baby boy takn 2 soonnnnnnn!"

The response had been immediate and overwhelming: messages to "stay strong" and "God needed another angel!!1!" and "RIP Brian! Sooooo sad!" and Carrie began to feel a swell of satisfaction that so many people were reaching out to her, thinking about her, wondering about her. And then someone posted on her wall "God, that's awful, what happened?" and Carrie posted a reply. "worst thing evaaaaaah!!!,,,I killed my own sweet baby Bri Bri,,,ran over him on accident,,,am soooooo sad,,,if only he hadn't been riding his big weel and not listening 2 me bcause I had told him 2 stay in the house,,,don't know how I can ever get over this terilbe accident,,,but

I know that gods will was 2 have Brian with him and god wants me 2 b strong,,,will post more later 2day and 2morrow,,,every1 stay tuned,,,XXOO Luv u all!"

She'd reread her new status over and over and it almost brought tears to her eyes. She was being so brave. But after she posted, a lot of the messages stopped coming. She was puzzled, but then decided that probably everyone was just waiting to see what she would post next. It was very dramatic–like a movie.

But now this lawyer was telling her to say her parents had done it. It would make her Facebook posts look stupid. Embarrassing.

"We can say my dad tried to poison him, but we have to say that I ran him over by accident," she'd said, staring intently at Thomas Evigan. He was very handsome. She wondered if he was probably going to fall in love with her. It would make the story even better, plus lawyers were rich and she'd love to be a rich lawyer's wife. She figured that they could have two kids, two beautiful children, and she'd be good to them. That would kind of erase everything that had gone wrong with the monster. Erase the little mistakes she'd made. Kind of a do-over.

Thomas Evigan tried to control his temper. He had to keep reminding himself that he didn't care whether he actually won the case or not. He knew this little cunt had killed her kid and in a really disgusting way, too. She deserved jail time and most likely, she'd get it. So he didn't mind if he lost, just as long as the trial lasted a good long while. Just as long as his name got out there. You couldn't buy that kind of advertising.

"Carrie, that doesn't make any sense. Don't you understand? Brian would have been sick, his shoulder dislocated; he wouldn't then run outside to Goddamn play. Can't you see that? He was in horrible fucking pain. The iodine was eating him from the inside out and I can't even imagine how the dislocated shoulder must have felt. Christ, it probably took his mind off his nausea and burning guts. At least, until you crushed his skull with your Stratus," he was shaking his head in disgust—disgust that she could be this dense. "We can't show that you had any involvement. We can only say that they forced you to cover for them. For their monstrousness. And listen, you have to get the crying thing worked out. Because I'm putting you on the stand."

Carrie liked the sound of that. She could picture it. She'd have to make sure she had a real handkerchief, she'd seen that somewhere. Or, wait, maybe Thomas Evigan should hand her his as she cried—he could take it from his pocket and hand it to her, his fingers lightly brushing hers—everyone would see that as the beginning of the two of them falling in love. He'd be her protector, her champion!

Thomas Evigan watched the little psychopath's face and could practically read word for word her thought process. Many of his female (and some of his male) clients had fallen in love with him. He thought he could use it.

"Hey, Carrie," he softened his voice and laid his hand over hers. "I'm here for you. Don't forget that, okay? Everything I am doing is to make sure you do not go to jail. I don't want you in jail. You understand that, right?"

He squeezed her hand.

* * *

The Devil cried more, the leaking tears making his head heavier, not lighter, as Thomas Evigan's thread in The Litany showed his manipulations: steering Carrie in his direction, getting enlargements of the pictures of Brian happy and alive and contrasting them with enlargements of the barely recognizable corpse, relishing the collapse of the cunt's parents as the trial went on and on, clipping each article from each paper, enjoying lunches with people he'd not otherwise have met so soon in his career, putting his foot firmly on this trial, his stepping stone, his leg up, his shoe grinding the tragic death of one small boy into nothingness. Crushing it into oblivion as he turned the attention away from the dead boy, turned the attention away from the heinousness of the crime, and threw enough mud and muck at the parents, the school system, the police, to mix up the jury.

Then something happened even he could not have expected—Carrie was acquitted.

When he heard the verdict from the Jury Foreman, it flashed across his mind that he had made a terrible mistake. That he'd given this psychopath free reign to go on and terrorize, even kill, another child. Maybe several children. He felt an instant of self-disgust so strong his face suffused with hot blood and bile rose to the back of his throat. A thought trailed over and over in his mind—a pronouncement, a damnation: he had offended. He had offended.

He had offended.

Tears rose to his eyes and it was foreign, so foreign, he'd not cried since he was, oh, three, maybe. Maybe four or five, but not as an adult. Never as an adult. He thought quickly, turned and swept Carrie into his arms, laying his face on her shoulder, making sure he was faced out, eyes closed and tears visible, and he knew the picture it would make. Knew how they'd run it front page, the only one who'd believed in her, the champion that had saved this innocent girl, a man so compassionate that he could not hold back his own overwhelming emotion at having, quite possibly, saved her life.

The Devil's head hung almost between his knees, overcome, worn down, done in, beaten. He remembered his life before as the Angel Lucifer: compassionate, understanding, loving, beautiful…but afraid. Afraid of Free Will and what humans would do with it, even as he felt the stirring of his own Free Will as it began to whisper of a place greater than that of God, Himself–and who should occupy that place.

And so he had become Satan: the Devil, Himself, monstrously ugly and stoic, and he'd punished and punished and punished, all according to what God, Himself wanted. But only after–after death, after the person had quite possibly gone on to wreak more havoc, after they'd stolen again and again, stolen property, or innocence, or even lives, after, always after.

The Devil waited until they died and then punished them equally, whether thief or murderer, blasphemer or zealot, and not minded until now. But there was something about Thomas Evigan, about his ambition, the trail of destruction he had wrought and would continue to wring into the future–and the Devil saw the pictures of the small body as Thomas Evigan saw them: exciting, publicity, a golden ticket–and the Devil was sickened. Would no one stand up for that little boy? Would no one stand up for right and punish those that had done wrong?

Would no one stand up?

Surely Thomas Evigan would be punished for his sins, but only after he had died, and that was the part the Devil could no longer abide. The Devil decided to mete out punishment in the here and now, not after Thomas Evigan had enjoyed fifty or sixty years of good dinners, expensive clothes, even more expensive whores, adulation, respect, and even love from a woman who would not see the monster in him and would bear his children and he would gaze upon his own children and never once would his mind go back to Brian, the unfortunate whose death he'd left unavenged.

The Devil knew he needed a body, a willing soul, so that he could walk the skin of the Earth and mete out a new punishment, according to his own judgment. He would do it just this one time and then come back to Hell. And he'd bring Thomas Evigan with him.

But what soul would be willing to allow the Devil entrance? No thief, murderer, adulterer, molester, greed monger, would ever be that self-sacrificing…they fought against possession even as they passed over. No, he needed someone who was choosing to pass. A person that gave up their life willingly would have no qualms about another being stepping into their place.

He closed his eyes, heavy-lidded and burning and searched The Litany, looking for a special circumstance, a certain set of criteria—his eyes rolled under his bulging eyelids like a dreamer caught in a nightmare of unimaginable horror. His lips pulled back from the double row of knife-sharp teeth so unruly they cut the inside of his mouth with each movement. Blood continued to pour from every inch of him, puddling on the damned, igniting, burning as they howled their chorus of eternal pain. Then he saw it: small and almost non-existent, barely causing a ripple on the line much less a spark; the meekest, most subdued of all the sins that make up The Litany: a suicide.

BOOK THREE

The Devil Stood Up

Mark Anders was played out.

At thirty-one, it had been sixteen years since he'd consumed his first drug and it had been six years since he'd gone more than a day without using. He was used up. Used. Mark had done everything imaginable to get the drugs his system had come to depend on. He'd stolen from family, friends and the occasional employer. He'd tricked himself out although that had become a lot less profitable as he'd gotten older and harder-looking. He'd even tricked out younger friends with the promise that he'd get them a fix.

A fix—it's the only thing there was. He didn't think about food except when he was falling-down faint with hunger, and he didn't think about the family that had adopted him, except for his little 'sister' Kelly who he still missed.

He for sure didn't think about the state of his soul and whether he'd damned himself to everlasting hell.

Just a fix. Always that.

He'd ended up here, on this dark, cold roof in Old City in Philadelphia. It was late and the breeze ruffled the trees, making the streetlights appear to sparkle—a nice area, but Mark didn't see nice. Mark saw only the fix that he couldn't get. Mark saw only the things he'd lost or given away willingly. Mark saw everything he didn't have. Mark saw it all in terms of anti, negatives, in the red, overdrawn, busted, used up, worn out, done.

"Mark?"

He turned from the low brick wall he'd been leaning against, looking out over the semi-dark parking lot of a theater. The people coming and going. The lives.

He turned and there was Kelly. Was it Kelly? He squinted and rubbed his arm over his eyes. It made him dizzy and a moment of vertigo tilted him back against the half-wall. He rounded his arms and tipped forward, stumbling.

"Mark!"

His gaze cleared and he saw that it was Kelly coming to him across the rooftop; she was eight and in her favorite cotton pjs with the ladybugs on them, then she was eleven and in bare feet and pigtails, and then she was seventeen with tears in her eyes as he left, bag packed, dad screaming at him; and then she was just Kelly, and he thinks she must be twenty-eight or -nine—was he thirty-one? Thirty-two? He couldn't remember for sure.

"Kell..." he said and swayed forward again. "Stop. Don't come any closer." He put his hand up, palm toward her. He shuffled backward and pulled himself onto the ledge of the half wall and crouched there, swaying.

"Mark, no!" she said and took a short step forward, clutching her hands under her breasts, light jacket belling out behind her from the wind. Her dark hair rose and snapped into her eyes and she put her hand up to hold it back.

"Stay back, stay right there," he said. "I'm sorry. I just wanted to see you and tell you to tell mom and dad that I'm sorry. And to tell you that I'm sorry."

"Mark, please," she said, tears coursing down her cheeks. "You don't have to do this. I forgive you, they forgive you. I know they do. Mark, they love you, we love you. We only want you to come home."

"It's too late, too late for me. I'm worn out. Sick of all of it," he stood and the wind buffeted him, molding his loose clothes to his stick-thin legs and arms.

A swell of pity ran through Kelly to see how wasted her brother's body had become. He looked as though he hadn't eaten in a month and he was dirty, so dirty. She could smell him from fifteen feet away.

"Mark, we can get you help, mom and dad want to help you. They'll pay to get you good treatment. It will work this time, I know it will. This is what they mean by rock bottom, isn't it? When they say you have to reach rock bottom before you can start—"

He cut her off with one quick shake of his head.

"I am so far past rock bottom that I can't even see it," he said, his voice was flat, quiet, but she had no trouble hearing him. The wind must have blown his words to her.

"Mark, please," she said, making her own voice calm, taking a step forward. "We can help you, it doesn't have to…"

He smiled, his teeth a jumble of yellow, crooked tombstones.

"Love you, Kell," he said.

He tipped on his heels, arms flung out like a kid falling into a pile of leaves, and dove backward from the ledge.

- - -

Tied into Mark's consciousness in The Litany, the Devil felt the lift and drop of his stomach as he tilted back, heels grinding against the grit of the ledge, and as Mark's body fell, the Devil rose to meet him.

They joined briefly at the moment of impact and Mark's last, startled thought: hey who are you? echoed over and over as his consciousness continued its descent into Hell.

The Devil felt Mark's body around him like a too tight suit. Used to his own bulk, the frail, featherweight limbs came as a shock. This body's chest was a band of tightness that refused to ease and the Devil struggled for breath, not knowing how, not knowing the key to make a human body run. Then Mark's body, seemingly of its own accord, unlocked its diaphragm and the Devil took his first, gasping breath as a human.

It hurt.

Everything hurt.

He opened his eyes.

He rolled onto his side, gasping, then onto his stomach. Vertigo rushed through him and he felt the street tilt and he closed his eyes. He breathed. When the dizziness passed, he pushed himself onto his hands and knees and rested again. Then he brought one knee up, foot on the ground. He braced his hand on his knee and took another deep breath, head hanging. He pushed his hand against his leg and dragged his other leg up, getting that foot, too, on the ground.

Groaning, sweating, and nauseous, the Devil stood up.

* * *

Kelly had stood frozen after her brother disappeared from sight. Her mind reiterated the same sentiment over and over: it can't be, it can't be, it can't be. She shook her head to dislodge the useless thought, unstuck her feet from the gravelly rooftop and ran to the ledge.

Too panicked to scream or to remember the phone in her pocket, she bent over the ledge and out into the night, looking down. She saw Mark, twelve stories down, laying half on the sidewalk and half on the street, arms flung wide.

She was filled again with pity and a terrible, grinding sadness that she associated with interactions concerning her brother. A part of her, very small but there, felt only resignation that he'd come to this kind of end. That part had known all along, it seemed, that this is where the track of Mark's life ended.

Then he stirred and she gasped, squinting down. Had she seen that? Was it just a trick of the dark and the wind blowing shadows over his corpse? But no, he shifted again, arms contracting in slightly, legs twitching, and she turned and flew to the stairs, still forgetting the phone in her pocket, thinking only to get to him as quickly as possible.

She pounded down the dark, piss-smelling stairwell, her hand gripping the railing, contracting and releasing with each bounding step. Her breath tore through her lungs. She finally reached the ground floor and banged through an emergency exit into the alley, a tired old alarm burring into life. She ignored the alarm and looked left and right, panting, trying to get her bearings.

She ran to the street side of the building, skidded around the corner and pulled up short. Mark was not there. She looked up and saw the ledge and knew she was in the right spot. She looked at the sidewalk again.

No Mark. She stood, dumbfounded, mouth hanging open.

* * *

The Devil was one block away, tucked into an alley, breathing heavily. He leaned against cold brick and tilted his head forward. This body ached and ached. He'd kept it from too much serious damage by meeting it at impact, but still...the body was in such bad shape to begin with. He coughed and blood splattered his shoes. This throat felt like it was tearing open. He coughed again and this time his diaphragm clenched and he threw up, trying to direct it away from himself, but not entirely successful.

"My brother just jumped from the top of...I don't know what it's called...the address is 901...yes, he jumped, and...no, I don't need an ambulance, I need the police, he's not...no, just the police, he got up, he got up and must have...I told you already, from the roof...I don't know, ten stories? Seven? I don't know, I'm not familiar with..."

The fretful, woman's voice was coming closer. He'd seen her, briefly, when he'd opened his eyes. She'd been staring down at him from the ledge. He assumed it was the ledge he'd jumped from. Who was she?

The Devil shook his head, clearing his mind: she'd said brother. It was the suicide's sister. And she was nearly to him.

He faded farther back into the alley, trying to be quiet, but this sick, clumsy body was not cooperating. Torrents of pain wracked it and the nausea was a continuous stream of torture, stirring his guts. Sick, this body was sick, but not just from the Transition. From the drugs, too. He'd have to find a place to lay up until he could get this body back to rights. Vertigo tilted the alley up and over him and he pinwheeled his arms but weakly, they were so weak. The vomit rose to his throat and he fell over, only semi-conscious. From far away but getting closer he heard:

"No it is not a joke, I am not drunk, my brother just…you have to send someone, you don't understand…"

The footsteps getting closer, seeming to ring like chimes in his ears, even as the voice seemed to fade away, float away. Floating…

Then he heard:

"Mark!"

And:

"Mark, are you all right? How did you…"

And after a little while:

"I'm bringing my car around. We'll get you to a hospital and…"

Then nothing more for another little while. He let this body drift, semi-conscious. It felt good to drift; it felt better.

Then the clunk of a car door and arms around him, trying to push him to sit up. He groaned, a trickle of vomit hot over his tongue and chin, and slitted his eyes open. She knelt before him, grunting and struggling, her dark hair hung untidily over her eyes and she flicked her head once, twice, to clear her sight. Her eyes were extraordinarily beautiful, a vivid emerald green that shone even in the small bit of streetlight that made it into the alley. He blinked. It reminded him of Heaven, where everything had been beautiful even without body, without mass such as here on Earth.

Her eyes were truly ethereal.

Now those eyes shifted to his and she paused in her tugging of his arms.

She smiled but the worried cast in her eyes would not dim.

"You'll be okay," she said.

And:

"I'm taking you to the hospital."

And:

"I can't believe you…"

Before she faded out again.

He awoke in the seat of a car and rolled his head left and she seemed to sense his eyes on her and she glanced at him. "We're almost there. If I can just get these one way streets figured out…"

She leaned forward, struggling to read the signs as they drove under the streetlights. Light swept gradually over her face and then away, as if a photographer trapped in a slower time had decided to take her picture.

"No," he said, rasping, swallowing. "No…hospital."

She looked over, startled.

"Yes, hospital," she said and turned back to navigate.

"No…I don't want…I can't…" he said, his voice trailing away into a cough.

"You are going to the hospital. Mark, you fell from the top of that building! You don't know what might be wrong inside. You could be bleeding internally or—"

"I didn't fall," he said.

Her jaw tightened.

"No. I know you didn't," she said.

"I'll do it…I'll just do it again…if you make me go there."

Anger flashed into her emerald eyes but was gone just as quick as it came, leaving resignation. Such sad, deep resignation that the Devil wondered briefly what she'd been through with this body, this man Mark, her brother. He could guess at some of it. He'd seen so much of

Mark's type in The Litany. But he'd never seen the other side of it, the consequences side. The loved one's side.

"Just take me home," he said and tilted his head back against the seat. The lights flashed faster, leaving bright spots on his retinas even under his closed lids. After a while, the tires bumped and then began to hum–they were on the bridge, heading out of the city.

The Devil tried to relax but the nausea was a constant discomfort and now this body was getting chills and fever, chills and fever, and he was overtaken by an enormous thirst. The streetlights ended and now they were in mostly unbroken darkness, not even another car on the road this early in the morning, and the Devil wondered if he'd made a grave error in choosing this body.

Then he dozed.

Beside him, Kelly was silently berating herself for falling for her brother's threats. She knew he should be in a hospital, but of everything he'd threatened in the past, he'd never threatened suicide.

She knew he hadn't called her last night in the hopes that she'd save him. He'd been determined to kill himself.

She hadn't heard from him for at least six months and when she'd answered the unknown number displayed on her cell phone, she hadn't recognized his voice at first. It was slurred but quiet, almost a whisper. He'd told her that he loved her and loved their parents and was so sorry for everything that had gone wrong. Everything he'd put them through.

She'd heard this before, heard all of this from him before, and was at first merely annoyed. This was part of his pattern: get wasted, get ecstatic, get sad, get depressed, and then, if he was still cogent (which wasn't very often, not by this point in the pattern), call sister and cry.

But it hadn't been the same. His voice hadn't been the same. He was calm, not hysterical. He wasn't crying or begging for anything…he'd sounded matter-of-fact. Sad, but determined to get said what he wanted to say. And then he'd hung up.

She'd been left with a pit in her stomach and a sudden certainty of what he was planning.

It was only luck that she'd found him.

Kelly was six when her parents adopted Mark. They had decided after five years and three miscarriages that adoption would be a less heartbreaking solution to expanding their family. They'd fallen in love with Mark the minute they'd laid their eyes on him. With his coloring, he even looked as though he could have been their biological child.

He'd been an orphan since he was four, and he'd been returned from two foster homes for behavioral issues by the time he was seven. Kelly's parents adopted him the day after he'd turned eight.

At the time of the adoption, they'd lived in the building Mark had fallen from. This was the first real 'home' Mark had known. He'd sit on the roof for hours and watch the theater next door. He liked to watch people trickle in by ones and twos and then after a time, pour back out in a busy crowd that blackened the sidewalk and quickly dispersed. Then the pattern would start all over again.

It had only been three years they'd lived there, but for Mark, they were the best three years of his life. He was learning to control his emotions and was starting to finally get over his fears of the unknown—of instability. Then, when Kelly's father had changed jobs, they'd moved to the suburbs.

It was in the suburbs of Central Jersey that Mark had first tried drugs. By his junior year he was addicted and had already been to three treatment facilities. He turned eighteen during his senior year and at his first arrest as an adult, his parents had let him sit in jail for a week. They were tired of the lies and stealing but even more so, they were tired of the abuse Mark heaped on them—and he did pile it on. He blamed them for everything. He told them they'd ruined his life by moving him away from everything he was familiar with. It was their fault he'd even tried drugs. Their fault he'd gotten hooked. Their fault he'd had to turn to theft to support his burgeoning habit.

None of it was his fault. He'd done nothing wrong, just been a victim of his parent's selfishness and self-centeredness.

Even at sixteen, Kelly had been smart enough to realize that everything Mark accused their parents of—especially the self-centeredness—were really things he despised about himself and therefore couldn't face. He couldn't take the responsibility. He was weak.

She glanced at him now, slumped against the car door. His mouth hung open, arms crossed over his thin chest. The darkness was not kind to his ravaged face. Deeply socketed, his eyes could have been the empty holes of a skull and his cheekbones stood out, shadowing the area below, reinforcing his skeletal appearance.

An almost physical weight seemed to settle around her. The lead-lined mantle of taking responsibility for him. Again.

She pulled into her driveway, bumping gently over the apron. The house was a small, tidy Cape Cod on a street lined with similar homes. There weren't yet any flowers in the beds, it was too early in the year, but she already knew she'd put impatiens, salvia, and snapdragons in the front beds and something trailing, ivy or bougainvillea, in the window boxes. Satisfaction settled her stomach and leeched some of the tension from her shoulders. It always felt good to be home. Like a little bit of Heaven.

She looked again at Mark and then opened her door. She got out and closed the door as quietly as she could—the houses here were close together and she didn't want to wake her neighbors.

The night had gotten very chilly. She checked the time on her phone—4:30. She'd have to call out of work today and maybe tomorrow, too. Depending on how sick Mark was this time. She stood for a minute more, listening to the silence, broken only by one lone truck swishing past on the distant highway.

She went to the passenger side and eased it open, pulling slowly in case he was leaning on it. As it opened, he pushed himself back and deeper into the seat.

"Mark," she said, whispering and laying a hand on his shoulder. Even his shoulder was bony.

"Mark," she said again, shaking him. "Come on, let's go in. Mark?"

He gasped as though she'd woken him in the middle of a nightmare. His eyes opened wide and he looked left to right. He brought his hands up near his chest, palms out, as if warding something off.

She squeezed his shoulder.

"Mark, we're home, come on out," she said and tried to smile. The night had been a little too long and difficult for her to produce anything near a real smile. It was more just a tired tightening of her lips.

His eyes found hers and he stared, looking dazed.

"Who are you?" he said.

Her lips tightened even more. Now that she'd been out of the car, she could smell how sour, almost rotten, the interior had become. Anger shot through her and she considered turning around and leaving him to fend for himself but the anger passed—she was probably too tired to sustain much anger—and she gripped his wrists and pulled him from the car. He was light, he couldn't weigh more than 135 or so, and that brought the pity back, but tinged with disgust. I guess I am still a little mad, she thought.

"Ha ha Mark, come on, quit messing around. I've had enough. Really."

He stood, swaying, and looked from her to the house.

"I'm so tired," he said.

She nodded.

"I know you are. Come on, let's get inside."

He shuffled after her and leaned against her back like an exhausted toddler as she unlocked the door.

In quick succession she felt: pity, disgust, anger, resignation.

The resignation always won out, in the end.

She opened the door, reached behind her for his hand, and led him in.

* * *

Two days.

For two days, the Devil struggled in this body he'd commandeered. For two long days it sweated and discharged matter from both ends. It ached, it twitched, its muscles contracted so painfully that the Devil was reminded of his own torturous limbs. It bucked and buckled and leaked fluid from every orifice. It stank. And it hurt.

Not once did the Devil think about giving this body over and finding his way back. Torturous as detoxing was, it paled in comparison to Hell.

Kelly called out of work for three days, pleading a family emergency. She didn't want to do it, but she had no choice. Watching Mark detox was almost as painful for her as it was for the Devil going through it. She wrestled a plastic sheet under him after he'd vomited for fifteen minutes straight, lying on his side the entire time. She wiped his face and put chapstick on his lips. She forced water on him sip by sip. She worried and she paced. She slept in a chair in the room with him, but never soundly, only drifting in and out as he grunted and groaned in agony.

She'd seen him go through this before, once at her parents, once here, and once she'd seen the beginning of it at the emergency room while he'd waited his turn to get his arm stitched where a bottle had cut it. The bottle had been wielded by one of his street friends on a bad trip. By the time the nurse took him back, his symptoms were obvious and after stitching him up they'd had him sent, via police car, to the closest treatment facility.

But she'd never seen him this way, never so…stoic. That was the only word she could think of for his behavior. Although tears of pain squeezed from his eyes, he never sobbed. He cried out, but only in grunts or groans, he never screamed for his fix. He didn't accuse her of keeping drugs from him. He didn't accuse her of holding him against his will. In fact, he didn't acknowledge her at all. This was a private battle he was fighting. And she thought that this time, he might make it.

He just seemed determined.

On the third morning, warm sun in her face woke her. She stretched in the chair, yawning, and realized she'd slept soundly. The room was silent. Mark was not in the bed. She had a sudden premonition that her front door would be hanging open, Mark long gone. Then she had another that she would find him, dead, on her bathroom floor.

She struggled out from under the light blanket she'd pulled over herself the night before and trotted barefoot to the front door. Closed and locked. She could see the bathroom from here. The door was open and sun lit the white tile to sparkling. And no one was in there.

There was a clink and she turned back down the hall into the kitchen. Mark was sitting at the little linoleum topped kitchen table, drinking coffee. Coffee grounds had spilled all around the coffee maker and onto the floor. He looked up when she came in. She stood and watched him, waiting for him to say something. But he said nothing, only tilted the cup to his lips and swallowed.

Anger and annoyance pulsed through her.

"Good?" she asked, putting her hands on her hips. Her kitchen was white and normally spotless. The cascade of grounds looked like crumbling offal.

He glanced at her again over the rim of the mug.

"It's nice here," he said. "Quiet. Warm but not hot. Not what I expected." His voice was raspy but calm.

She blinked. Had he lost his mind? Had the fever cooked his brain?

"Mark, what's wrong with you? You don't sound—"

"I'm hungry," he said, as though that would explain his oddness. But it only reinforced her feeling that he was acting strangely. Mark never asked for food. For him, food was beside the point.

She brought her fingertips to her forehead and rubbed lightly in small circles and closed her eyes.

"You're annoyed when you do that," he said.

She looked up and caught the puzzlement that flashed across his face. Almost as though he didn't know why he'd said what he said.

"Yes, Mark, I'm annoyed. It looks like a gorilla made coffee. Or, no! Not even a gorilla, they're really smart—something that doesn't have thumbs…a dog or a bear, maybe! It's the only thing that could explain coffee grounds spread over every inch of my kitchen."

He turned and looked behind him then back to her.

He said nothing and sipped from his mug again.

She sighed and pulled out the chair opposite him, letting her hand rest on the reassuringly cool tabletop. If he was going to be exasperating then she'd just have to ignore it.

"How do you feel?" she asked, making her way to the coffee pot, stepping gingerly across the mess. She pulled her hair back with a tie she'd pulled from her pocket.

"There is some clarity now, to my thinking. This brain functions well enough." He watched her and noted her plain face, her capable hands, and a series of purple scars that began at the base of her skull and ran down below the line of her shirt.

She raised her eyebrows and glanced back at him as she poured coffee into a mug.

"Oooookaaaaay," she said, coming to the table. "Whatever that means."

"You have scars," he said.

"Um…yeah. From the accident, Mark, you know that," Embarrassed anger flitted quickly over her features. Anger at him, embarrassment for him.

He turned his head to stare out the window over the sink. The trees in the back yard had a light green haze—the buds of new leaves. The sky was light blue and cloudless. It would get darker blue as the season changed to summer and then to fall.

The Devil had never occupied a human body and was surprised to realize he'd somehow retained a bit of 'Markness', a hint of his memories. But they were hazy. Well buried. Mostly inconsequential.

He could find nothing of the accident of which she spoke.

"So, tell me something, Mark," Kelly said, looking into her mug. "What happened? Why did you do it?"

"Do what?" he asked, turning back to her.

She sighed and set her mug down.

"This coffee is terrible. You used to be able to make coffee," she said and shook her head. Then she looked into his eyes. "Why did you jump off that building? Why did you try to kill yourself?"

He turned to gaze out the window and she considered him. He wasn't nervous, he wasn't manic but also he wasn't depressed. He just seemed calm. And sure. And she'd never have associated those words with her brother, even during his 'clean' times.

"Mark, what happened to you?" she asked and he turned back to her.

His eyes, green like her own, were full of a deep sadness that took her aback. There was nothing self-pitying or victimish in the sadness, there was only something she recognized from her own face in the mirror: resignation.

"I know you think I'm your brother," he said, his words slow and deliberate like someone stepping carefully through dangerous territory, considering the wisdom of each step before it's made. "But I am not. Your brother is dead."

Kelly's first, startling thought was yes, I thought so but she pushed that aside. What the heck did that mean? Mark was right here in front of her, not dead. Of course he wasn't dead. He was just being…Mark.

She nodded and sipped her coffee.

"Whatever, have it your way, you're not my brother, okay?" she said and raised her eyebrows at him. "So, Mister Complete Stranger, why did you toss yourself off that building?"

"No, you misunderstand," he said. "Your brother did jump from that building and he did kill himself. But I am not your brother." His face was calm, his voice patient. It shook her that he was so still. Mark was normally a mass of twitches, jokes, sarcastic remarks, finger-snapping, arm-waving–everything about him kinetic.

But now he sat immobile and considered her with composed green eyes, his hands calm on his mug. It was scaring her.

"Okay, I get it," she said. "You don't want to talk about it right now. Fine, fine! Whatever. We can talk about it later."

He gazed at her a moment longer and she felt heat creeping into her cheeks. Then he turned back to the window. Without looking at her he said: "I'm very hungry."

* * *

She cooked for him and he ate. He ate eggs, bacon, and toast and wasn't satisfied, so she made him potatoes, too, fresh grated and fried with a little chopped onion, and he ate them too and wasn't satisfied so she cut up a chicken she'd been saving for the weekend and she fried the chicken and he ate that, too, and finally seemed satisfied. His stomach stuck out from his bony frame.

They had talked very little.

Kelly was confused. She couldn't shake the feeling– every time her back was to him–that it wasn't her brother sitting at the table. It looked like him, but didn't sound like him, didn't act like him. It isn't him her mind insisted that's not your brother and she told herself she was crazy, that it was just the power of suggestion, that she just hadn't seen him in a very long time…but nothing could convince that voice of doubt in her mind.

She turned from the sink where she'd piled the dishes as she'd cooked. He was rubbing his stomach and staring out the window again. He looked a bit uncomfortable. No wonder, she thought, half my kitchen is in his stomach!

"Are you staying here tonight?"

The Devil wondered at this woman's love for her brother even after two days of him vomiting and pissing the bed. Even after tearing himself so violently from the face of the Earth. Was there nothing that would stop her loving her adopted sibling?

"Is it just because you are siblings?" he asked. "Is that the reason? Or is it something in you specifically?" He tilted his head inquiringly as he considered her. She was plain of feature, only her eyes elevated to the realm of beauty. And she was very alone; the Devil knew that. He knew it from this too-silent house so carefully and meticulously maintained.

She was shaking her head, arms folded over her chest.

"Mark, I don't know what you want from me, I really don't. Of course it's because you're my brother. I'll always love you. Even when you are acting the jackass. As you are now."

He blinked and then a slow smile spread across his lips. He nodded.

"I think it is more about you; something in you. The ones that come to me…they are weak. Weak in their minds and weaker still in their wills. But not you," he said. He considered her again, head tilted in an oddly un-Mark-like way. "You are very strong. Very determined. Very strong-willed."

Pleasure slipped through her like balm, soothing her tired nerves. How long had she waited for some acknowledgement from him? But she only shook her head again. The feeling that this was not Mark was still clamoring in the back of her mind, but getting louder, coming to the fore.

"Mark, listen…"

"I am not Mark. I am not your brother," the Devil said, his voice calm but very, very firm.

"Okay, fine, you're not Mark, even though you look just like him and we've been together since you…fell or jumped or whatever from that building two days ago. Fine. You're not my brother," she said, arms tightening at her chest. Her body had tensed, as if readying itself for a blow. She couldn't get her fingers to unclench. She felt like stone. "Who are you, then?"

"Kelly," he said, "I am the Devil."

Christine Dougherty

BOOK FOUR

The Devil Set Out

The Devil stood in the driveway of Kelly's Cape Cod and raised his head to the cool, almost cold, morning breeze. He checked the pockets of his jacket. The jacket was of jean material and so worn it had turned white at the stitching. It was comfortable if a little too big; the sleeves hung to the backs of his hands. It was old and the barely legible tag said GAP. Kelly had bought this jacket for Mark for Christmas, 1998. Too long ago, now.

A thin wallet with his ID and one debit card were in his left hand breast pocket. The wallet was new. Kelly had given it to him in her kitchen that morning.

She'd driven to Mark's apartment (which she paid the rent on) the night before to retrieve some clothes and found the jacket hanging forlornly in the front hall closet. The only jacket Mark had, even through the winter months. She'd grieved, standing in the apartment, holding his jacket to her chest.

She'd grieved his passing.

She'd been standing at the sink, arms crossed and getting pissed when he'd made his claim that he was the Devil. She'd felt the straw that would break her camel's back fluttering inches away. She couldn't figure out if he was being self-pitying or what the deal was but he sure hadn't had Mark's signature 'why do bad things always happen to me?' look.

And then he'd motioned for her hand.

She'd shaken her head, no way, even as her arms unclenched and she stepped one step and then two, her mind screaming at her body to stop, stop, what the hell are you doing? Don't go near him, he's the Devil! The God damned Devil!

Foolishness, the rational part of her brain insisted, total foolishness. It's just Mark being Mark. If you take his hand, he'll just do something dumb like pull his hand away at the last second and slap yours, so don't, whatever you do, take his hand. It's not a good idea. Not a good idea at all.

She realized the rational and irrational parts of her mind may have been at odds over the why of it, but neither side wanted her to touch that hand that hung so calmly, five feet away.

And she told herself that she wouldn't take his hand.

She would refuse.

She took another step. And another. And then her hand was in his.

She stared into his green eyes, almost a mirror to her own but older and more worn, and she felt her hand growing warm. Not as though he was transferring heat to her, his hand did not feel hot at all; in fact, his hand seemed to get cooler the hotter hers became. She looked at their linked hands, searching for the source of the heat and there was none and then she looked back into his face. His eyes were gone and where they had been was a jumble of flame and blackened husks turning and turning on the heat waves, never completely out of contact with the nimble fire.

Her body was so hot, sweat began to form at her hairline and one small drop slipped loose and slid into the corner of her eye, stinging. Her mouth hung open and was going dry as though she were breathing scorched dessert air.

She couldn't turn her gaze from those husks. They looked dense and heavy but somehow they floated, buffeted and turned and then she saw agony on one even though it was faceless, nameless, a mass of heavy, writhing something but nothing. She heard agony from another and then another, fading in and getting louder. Moans of pain. Cries of torment. She felt it as a sound deep in her mind, mid-brain or deeper, almost as though these tormented souls were in her.

Her head was getting hotter. She felt her brain was beginning to boil in the bowl of her cranium and she became afraid. She did not want to burn.

For the husks, or souls, or whatever they were, she felt

a pity so deep that it was beyond tears, beyond grief. It was a stern, unbending emotion that said it is not good…but it is right.

Then one of the husks turned slowly, buffeted to the fore of her sight, and she had recognized her brother. She didn't know how she had recognized him; all the husks were heavy, burning replicas of each other. But somehow, she knew. She knew that one in particular was Mark. And he was burning.

The Devil dropped her hand and instantly her body returned to normal except for the sweat that had formed under her hair. No heat, no flames in his eyes, no souls crying in her mind. She stood staring in shock at what had been Mark.

Then she'd believed.

Oh yes, she'd believed all of it.

And then she'd fainted.

The Devil had carried her to her room and laid her in the bed. He'd retrieved the thin blanket from the guest room and bloused it out and over her. He was pleased at the way the fine material floated, weightless and fluttering at its edges, like white wings.

Then he had studied her still, pale face. She had found pity in herself for the sea of the damned. Not understanding, not agreement or disagreement with the punishment–just pity. Her pity was not born of weakness, either; the Devil had understood that at once as he'd traveled with her to hell. Her pity was a product of her strength. Of her will.

The Devil, himself had never felt pity for the damned he punished.

When she woke, she'd been calm but dazed, almost shocky. She'd had a difficult time looking at Mark, because his outside was so very much the same but his insides…so very much not. The beginnings of grief were stirring in her as she remembered, over and over, that Mark had been there. In hell.

Poor Mark.

She was anxious for the Devil to go. He'd told her he had business here on earth and she had nodded, but the strain of what she'd learned subdued any curiosity she might have been able to muster in regards to his…business.

She was anxious for him to go so she could gather herself back together. She saw the possibility of it, but it was vague and far off. Something she'd need to work toward.

So she'd retrieved Mark's belongings for him (the Devil) but had been unable to turn over Mark's old leather wallet with his initials carved into it. Mom and dad had given him that wallet on his eighteenth birthday. Instead she'd stopped at a men's store and bought him this new one, thin and crisp, and put Mark's ID and her own debit card in it.

"You'll have to answer to Mark, Mark Anders," she'd said on the morning he was to take his leave. He was slipping on the jean jacket and putting the wallet (the new wallet) in his front breast pocket. She was sitting at the kitchen table, staring at her hands clutched loosely in front of her. "I'll add your name to my bank account this morning so you shouldn't have any trouble with the card. You should be all set." She'd glanced up and a small, tense smile ran across her lips and was gone. Then she'd looked back down at the table, so terribly confused by her own motivations. She knew this was not her brother, but his appearance…she couldn't get past it.

The Devil had laid a hand on her shoulder and she'd smiled the small, tense smile again, but hadn't looked at him. Couldn't look at him. He'd gone to the front door and stepped into the cool early morning.

Now he stood in the driveway and checked his breast pocket one more time. The highway was his destination. He'd refused the offer of Kelly's car. He wouldn't be needing it.

He looked back at the house and felt a disturbing wave of reluctance to leave. The house glowed in the early morning sun, the white siding clean and the black shutters crisp and straight. Kelly had painted her front door a striking, fire engine red. The flowerbeds were bare but fresh black mulch had been piled in them and they looked anticipatory; ready for this new season and the flowers that Kelly would plant in a few weeks.

The Devil understood that—charming as it was—it was not the house he was reluctant to leave.

It was the woman, Kelly, whom made him reluctant to go away.

He turned away from the house and shrugged, trying to slough off the feeling. Following Kelly's directions, he set out for the highway.

He walked and paid attention to the fatigue that was already settling into these weak, worn out muscles. Even the pack he'd shrugged onto his back, light as it was, started his thin shoulders aching and twisted a hot knot of pain between his shoulder blades before he'd gone one mile. And he felt hungry, his stomach knotting and growling.

The Devil came upon the highway. It was two-lane, rural, bound on both sides by trees and further down he could see farmland. He was in New Jersey, not too terribly far from Philadelphia, where he thought he would find the lawyer, Thomas Evigan. He wasn't privy to The Litany anymore, and though it was a profound relief, it also served to cut him off from the path Thomas Evigan had taken.

The Devil stood at the edge of the highway and in the

distance, saw a vehicle coming from the direction he did not want to go and in the direction he did. He shrugged the pack from his back, relieved to feel cool air where the straps had dug mercilessly into this body's shoulders.

He waited.

As the vehicle approached, the Devil felt a building anticipation, which he at first attributed to his mission begun. But as he stood there, the anticipation bloomed larger and larger, unfurling like a heavy, black blossom, taking up all the space for this body's breath, and this skull began to hum as if filled with a large, poisonous wasp, and the Devil realized he might know who was coming.

The vehicle came around a shallow curve and was fully in view. It was a sunshine yellow 1954 Ford F-100 pickup truck, the front painted in flames so vibrantly red and orange they shimmered as if with actual heat. The truck was a dandy, and would have brought a smile to any man's lips.

But the Devil did not smile.

The truck slowed to a stop twenty feet from where he stood. Early morning sun glimmered and flashed across the windshield, hiding the driver. The engine idled, rumbling powerfully, a growl that would make any man smile.

But the Devil did not smile.

The engine revved and the truck jumped, playfully, like a tiger cub grown to monstrous size. Then it jumped again, tires chirping on the blacktop.

It was now fifteen feet from the Devil and it jumped a third time, gaining another five. Laughter, chuckling and thin and somehow sardonic, slipped from the open windows of the cab, and the truck jumped again, pulling dead even with the Devil.

The driver leaned over and popped the passenger side door, which yawned wide, barely missing the Devil where he stood. Leaning across the seat, the driver smiled and the smile sat uncomfortably under his jet-black mop of hair and black, sparkling eyes. This man's thin lips seemed more prone to a sneer than a smile.

"Aye, well, sure and begorrah, if it idn't ta Divil, hissownself," he said, his Irish accent so broad it became a caricature; an unflattering one, at that. "Coom ahn oop, Lucifer, an ryde along wit me." He put his fingers to the rim of the tight, plaid cap that had just appeared on his head and once again his laughter slid forth, mean-spirited and emaciated.

He put his hand out, his smile coiling tightly, a rattlesnake ready to strike…and the Devil took the proffered hand and allowed himself to be pulled into the cab. The passenger door swung shut of its own accord and the pick-up roared, tires screaming against the road, a cloud of blue black building behind it, and shot off in the direction the Devil had wanted to go.

* * *

"It's been a long time, Am," the Devil said.

Amon looked askance at his passenger and grinned. The cap had disappeared.

"Aye, that is has, laddie, that it has," he said. "Ye art soorly missed…" his grin widened, "…doon below."

The Devil said nothing, only gazed calmly out his window and kept his mind serene. He knew he could not show weakness in the face of this demon—most likely the first of many. But the Devil did not trust this borrowed junkie's body to do right by him, if worse should jump nimbly to worst. Amon was not the strongest of demons and if they'd met in Hell, the Devil would not have considered him an equal. But Amon was a demon nonetheless, and the demons who'd spent ample time with the humans were the most conniving of all.

And Amon had spent much of his time on Earth, leading the guilty further astray.

"You're looking pretty thin…and weak," Amon said, tsking and shaking his head. All traces of an accent had faded from his speech. "That body doesn't look like a keeper, to me. Think it'll stand up, Lucifer?"

The Devil never turned, only continued to watch the passing scenery, seemingly unperturbed.

"Let's cut to the chase, Am," he said. "And stop calling me Lucifer."

"Cut to the chase? Oh, my dear Lucifer, that is a funny one you found! Cut to the chase! Must have watched their fair share of action movies, I guess," Am said and then his voice took on a cozy, sycophantic edge, the accent back, but threading in and out, appearing and disappearing. "Odd isn't it? How you get a slight taste of the person who'd occupied the body before ye? Tempts you to want a new one every day, aye, laddie?"

Once again, the Devil said nothing, only turned to regard Amon with passive, emerald eyes.

Amon sighed, tilting his head back and rolling his eyes heavenward, drawing it out and giving it full weight and measure, making his exasperation theatrical and obvious.

"You know why I'm here, Lucifer," he said. "You're wanted back in Hell. I imagine you can guess who decreed it. Things are getting funky down there."

"They're burning, same as always. Nothing is going to change if I'm gone for a time."

Amon shook his head. "No, no, no, that won't do…what is Hell without Satan? You're needed down there, laddie. Your business is not here, it's there. You can't slum up here with us…you're much too important. Management says so, aye?"

"Is that so?" the Devil turned and raised his eyebrows at Amon, politely inquiring. "Who in management?"

"You know who, you know very well who," Amon said and his tone had lost its teasing quality. His words came out sounding like a jangle of twanged nerves.

"Can't even say His name, my dear?" the Devil asked, allowing the sarcasm full weight and measure. "Can't even say 'God, Himself'? Afraid it will stick in your throat, Am?"

Anger flashed across the demon's face and his thin lips thinned even more.

"Why are you even doing this, Lucifer? Rumor has it that it's because of some lawyer? Can that be right?" Amon was shaking his head. "When I first heard, I didn't believe it, couldn't believe it! Satan, Himself come up from hell to collect a soul? Unimaginable! Even we, Legion, do not presume in the sight of…the sight of…" he trailed off, shaking his head again. "Even we, Legion, would not take a soul. Not without…without…"

The Devil shook his head, a smile playing on his lips.

"You really can't say it? Still? After all this time?"

Amon's face reddened with rage and his head seemed to be melting, reforming, pushing itself out of shape. "I can say it! I can say it! God! God! God!…" he screamed, saliva spraying from his mouth and stippling the windshield as shimmering black feathers and a yellow beak grew from his features. "God! Gaw! Gaw!" He continued, his eyes shrinking to small, wet black dots surrounded by a somehow sickly, sunshine yellow. "Caw! Caw! Caw!"

The Devil threw his head back and laughed, liking the way the laughter loosened his belly and soothed his nerves, somehow drawing strength into this weak human form.

Amon's head snapped up and down and became human again, beak and feathers disappearing in an instant.

"Funny! Funny stuff, asshole!" Amon said, his temper and patience shot.

The Devil wiped tears from his eyes, still smiling.

"Amon, you're a tool; you always were. Why are you even here?" the Devil said, turning to Amon with a smile.

"Why am I here? Why?" Amon shrieked, reached across and gripped the Devil's arm, his grip like iron. "Because I'm taking your ass back to Hell, that's why!"

The old Ford had been going faster and faster and now Amon jerked the steering wheel one handed, and the truck peeled sharply to the left. They screeched across both lanes, turning sideways, sending the Devil crashing into the passenger side door, but still Amon kept a steady grip on his arm. The skinny wheels hitched, hitched again, and then caught, sending the truck end over end. It flipped and flipped again, smashing first the passenger side, then the roof, against the blacktop. It bounced again and now the driver's side smashed into the road and slid, gouging long furrows.

Amon held his seat and gripped the wheel with one straining hand, teeth pulled back in a grimace. With each bounce his head changed, becoming that of a wolf…a crow…a dog…changing with split second, blurring speed. Black feathers fluttered out the open driver's side window, coming to rest on the blacktop behind them.

The Devil braced himself, pushing his legs against the floorboards, one arm against the dash and one against the roof. He didn't bother with trying to dislodge Amon's hand, there wasn't time to fight him. If this body were to be killed, or Amon's body was killed while they were still linked, he'd have to start all over again and who knew if that would even be possible now that God, Himself had caught wind of this disobedient trek.

He drew from the remembered strength of his Satan form, forcing this body according to his will, making the muscles rigid, making it hold on. Minute tears rippled across his muscles and the Devil felt a return of pain, so like the bound and aching limbs of his Satan form, so like it in fact that it was almost comfortable.

And so he strained, sweating, teeth gritted, and held

this body in place, tearing muscle and tendon but holding, holding on as the truck flipped. Now slowing, now coming to rest, rocking, metal screeching and protesting and then becoming still, flat on the passenger's side door, groaning and ticking.

The Devil relaxed all the torn and aching muscles in this body and let it go limp in a heap against the door, realizing that Amon's hand must have left him at some point in the dizzying flips of the truck. He found he could not even lift his arm, could not shift his legs, could not turn his head to look for Amon.

He must find where Amon had ended up, because he wasn't in the cab of the truck any longer.

Forcing himself, ignoring the throbbing protests of this body, he turned over and wormed his way out the opening for the windshield. The glass glittered and crunched beneath him as he dragged himself out and into the sunlight. He drew his hands under his shoulders and pushed, forcing this body up and scrambled his feet under himself, groaning, not even aware that he groaned.

Amon sat cross-legged on the shoulder, watching the Devil drag himself from the ruins of the Ford.

"Hey, Lucifer," he said.

The Devil looked up, hands on his knees, panting. He ran the back of his hand across his mouth, drawing a line of blood across his chin to just under his ear. He noted how Amon shimmered, becoming indistinct, his head seeming to fade into that of a wolf…a dog…a crow, but slowly, almost dispiritedly.

The Devil could see the trees Amon sat in front of, could see right through him to the road he sat on.

"Yeah?" he said.

"I thought I had you for a second there. I should have held on, myself." Amon had kept the Devil pinned in the junkie's borrowed body with the touch of his hand. But it had also served to make his one-handed grip on the truck too precarious to withstand the force of the crash.

"Guess I'll see you in Hell, huh?" Amon said, and glanced to the back of the truck.

The Devil followed his glance and saw the body Amon had occupied, torn almost in two, innards strewn across the road. He looked back at Amon.

"Yeah, sure, Amon," the Devil said and now he, too, sat, resting his back against the side of the pickup, facing the specter on the shoulder. "Want me to wait with you?" the Devil said, knowing the shift could be a lonely business. Even a demon felt lost during the Transition between two states.

Amon shook his head, black feathers glimmering, but faintly, faintly.

"I'll see you down there soon enough," he said.

The Devil shook his head. "Not if I see you first, asshole."

Amon laughed, fading more, his laugh barely audible. His lips moved again, but the Devil couldn't hear what he said. He shook his head at Amon and a look of discomfort—almost fear—washed over Amon's borrowed features. He waved his arm in a 'go on, get out of here' gesture and turned away, huddling closer over himself.

The Devil gazed at Amon's transparent back for a moment more and then pushed this body to stand. He bent and fished into the cab, drawing forth his now battered backpack. Grimacing, he slipped it over his shoulders and let it come to rest on his back.

His mission was not well-begun.

As he walked away, his feet kicked up the black feathers that had fluttered to the road. They floated up and as they did, they, too, began to disappear. The Devil snapped his fingers at the puddle of gas seeping from the pickup and it burst into flames that ran hungrily toward the ruined truck. The cartoonish, painted flames on the hood and sides meshed and became one with the real flames until everything began to blacken indistinguishably. Then the truck, too, began to fade away into nothing.

The Devil was aware that Amon had turned to stare at the blackening truck, but he couldn't bring himself to look at Amon again.

He didn't want to see the despair on that demon's face.

* * *

He walked. He fished in his front pant pocket and pulled out a battered flip phone—it had been Mark's, the junkie. The Devil considered the phone in his hand and Kelly passed through his mind, her head bent over her folded hands, her mind a swirl of grief and a deep, soul-shaking unease. Unease that he had caused. He put the phone away.

This body ached with each step and blood had dried on his chin like a reddish-brown haze of beard stubble. Not much chance of getting a ride when he looked as though he'd quite possibly just eaten someone. He considered his feet, which ached, and wished he wasn't bound so much by the confines of this human form. He couldn't even relocate himself—say, to Philadelphia—without the possibility of dropping straight back to Hell if there wasn't a dying sinner available in the precise time and place he'd need it to be there. Without access to The Litany, it was a crapshoot.

He thought more about the trial that had taken place four years ago.

The prosecution had hammered the jury with expert testimony relating to what the last hour of Brian's life must have been like. The sickness he'd had from being poisoned, the terrible pain and stomach cramps. The nausea a dislocated shoulder could cause, taxing his already overtaxed stomach. The blinding, grinding pain of a dislocated shoulder. The brutality of a car bumper first hitting his shoulder and head and then bending his body back against the big-wheel seat, crushing and smothering. Then breaking his back and the car's tires rolling over first his left leg then his left arm. She must have checked then, the defendant, to see if he was dead but he wasn't, not yet. She must have then turned his body, jerking it into place under the tire, callously disregarding the blood, his shattered spine and flattened limbs, because then the car had gone forward, crushing his little mid-body, ruining everything inside him.

The members of the jury had paled and then gone paler still at each 20 by 24 photo the prosecutor erected on easels facing the jury box. By the time the coroner was finished testifying, there were no less than seventeen easels bearing up under their weight of photographic horror.

Seeing those sour cream faces, the prosecutor had been sure, had been certain, that Carrie would receive a guilty verdict and then the sentencing would begin. And the state would ask for death.

But it hadn't happened that way. The defense lawyer, Thomas Evigan, had somehow pulled a rabbit from his ass and gotten her acquitted. The rabbit—a shocking piece of testimony from a transient who said he'd seen the defendant's mom behind the wheel of the defendant's car that morning—was disgusting. It was covered in shit and half dead from suffocation, but there it was, and it cast just enough doubt among the jury—who knew the death penalty would be asked for—to set Carrie free.

Now, the Devil was going to pull another rabbit from Thomas Evigan's ass. And this rabbit would be in the form of his spinal cord and everything that God, Himself had packed so neatly into his ribcage. Then he'd let the shit fall where it may.

He considered what Amon had asked him. Why was he doing this? Why—after everything, after all the evil he'd been privy to? What made this lawyer different?

The Devil continued to walk. The morning sun was becoming the mid-morning sun and it warmed his shoulders. It was true that he'd seen worse evils, evils treacherous enough to break the most stouthearted of humans. And it was true that he'd been impassive and punished each with the same measure, doing the bidding of God, Himself—doing what God, Himself had decreed he must do for eternity or until God, Himself wiped him out completely or carried him back to Heaven.

The Devil swung his arms and clenched and unclenched his fists, feeling the muscles knitting busily back together, the tendons reattaching themselves to the bones. The ache was a constant torment, but bearable.

It was the willfulness, he decided. The sheer willfulness of Thomas Evigan to look at that dead baby boy and see in that little corpse a career boost. Not even a life-changing career boost, but a mere stepping-stone.

The willfulness.

That was what was so…

A car was coming up behind him.

This time, he did not turn. He felt none of the itching recognition of his own kind, his own kin. He continued his musings and as the car drew closer he wondered if following this path of thought might not lead him to a thicket impossible to tear himself free of. Let the humans examine and equivocate, searching their souls (more often to find an excuse for their misdeeds rather than perform the actions that would land them surely at salvation's gate) and morbidly pouring over and over their motivations.

He, the Devil, would punish this man now, on Earth, and then send Thomas Evigan where he belonged without the benefit of the sixty-odd intervening years he might otherwise enjoy…because it would please the Devil to do so.

It would please Him greatly and that was enough.

The car pulled to the shoulder behind him.

The Devil turned and at first he could not see the driver but then she leaned forward, her face coming into the light and it was Kelly.

Her face was set and pale, almost grim. She opened her door and stood, keeping the door between herself and the Devil. Her fear came off her waves.

"I…I'm glad I found you…I wanted to ask, to offer, I mean, I wanted to offer…" she swallowed and the Devil heard the dry, uncomfortable click even from ten feet away. He said nothing.

She lowered her head and her shoulders rounded as she took a deep breath. Then she looked up and into the Devil's (her brother's) eyes.

"I wanted to offer you a deal," she said, nodding slightly as if to say, yes, that's right, you heard me.

The Devil was familiar with the term 'deal with the Devil' because it was a constant undercurrent in The Litany. He did not take it lightly, especially from this woman who had never even once gotten herself tangled in The Litany. He considered her with impassive eyes.

"What deal would that be?"

Fresh fear flashed in Kelly's eyes and then she firmed her lips and lifted her chin.

"I want him back. My brother, Mark. I'll help you with your…mission or quest…or whatever it is…if you let him come back when you're done. When I've done enough."

He inclined his head toward her, considering her from

beneath half lowered lashes. His voice softened almost to a whisper.

"Have you never heard that the Devil is the father of lies, Kelly?"

She blinked rapidly but then nodded.

"I have heard it, of course I have. But not...you're not...I mean, this is going to sound insane, but..." She blushed a bright pink that warmed her features, softening the rigid lines of fear. Her words wound down in confusion.

"Continue," the Devil said.

"Okay, it's just that..." she said and gathered her wildly pinging thoughts, gripping the top of the driver's side door. "I don't think you're a liar. I don't think you're like we were taught. I don't think you're...evil."

The Devil nodded, considering. Then he said:

"I'm here to kill someone," he said and smiled. "Did you want to help me with that?"

* * *

He sat across from her at a diner. He had eaten a lot of food. Kelly is a little awed by how much he was able to put down. Mark had never been a good eater, at least not since drugs had become his main sustenance. It was unnerving to watch Him (she couldn't bring herself to think of him as 'The Devil' even though she knew it was true) occupying her brother's body but behaving in such an un-Mark-like way.

"Anything else?" the waitress asked, eyeing the four decimated plates in front of the dark-haired man. She hoped these people were twenty-percenters. It would make her lunch shift.

Kelly raised her eyebrows at the Devil, but he merely stared out the window into the parking lot and rubbed his stomach.

"No, I think we're good," she said to the waitress, the barest hint of a smile crossing her features.

"You all right, honey?" the waitress asked. She would not normally have been so forward, especially when she was this close to getting the customer up and out, but there is a deep shadow of grief in this plain woman's eyes. She senses that it has something to do with the man that sits across from her, now staring unconcernedly out the window.

The waitress has served hundreds, maybe thousands, of people, and she's usually quick to sort out who is who, but she isn't sure of these two. No wedding rings. They didn't speak much while they ate (well, while he ate, the lady only had coffee and a Danish) but that could just as easily be an indicator of marriage as not. There is a bit of a resemblance, they could quite possibly be related, siblings or maybe cousins. But the waitress had observed that the lady could barely meet the man's eyes but if she had, she might have seen what the waitress saw there: an odd mixture of curiosity, tenderness, and sorrow.

If she had to guess, she would have said that the man loved the lady but that the lady was longing for someone else.

"I'm fine," Kelly said. "Thank you."

The waitress nodded and put the check down between them and started to gather the plates. She did so in silence. As she turned to go, dishes stacked on her tray, she glanced at the man and he was staring at the lady again, but she has her eyes on her purse as she digs for her wallet and never looks up.

Wish someone would stare at me like that, she thought, and smiled a little. Her husband Roger would give a piece of his mind to anyone staring at her, although after twenty-six years of marriage, he was long past staring at her himself. He was still jealous, though, and not even tempered at all. She had the bruises to prove it.

Kelly got into the driver's seat and keyed the ignition as the Devil let himself in next to her. He groaned, sinking into the seat. Not really sure why, she finds herself getting angry. Maybe it is the misuse of her brother's body or the callous way he'd taken it over, but the flood of her anger overflows its banks.

"What are you groaning about? Why are you even in

this car? Can't you just…I don't know…fly or blink yourself to your destination or something? You're the Devil, aren't you?" She was so angry she turned the ignition key again, forgetting that the car was already running. It grinded shrewishly at her and then stalled and the check engine light glowed into being. "Darn it!" she said and hit the steering wheel.

His head was back against the seat, his eyes closed. He continued to rub his visibly distended stomach.

"Doesn't work like that. I wish it did," he said without opening his eyes.

"Well, I don't get it, I really don't," she said. Her voice was peevish and she twisted the key from the ignition. She would give it a second and then try again. "I mean, you should be able to do anything. Anything you want. Shouldn't you?"

"It doesn't work like that. Not from what I've heard, anyway," he said.

She looked at him and saw her brother's face, her brother's body. His eyes were still closed and his voice is slightly muffled as if he might fall asleep.

"What does that mean?" she asked. "What you've heard? Heard from who? None of this makes any sense at all…" her voice was rising, ignited by her anger. Beside her, the Devil opened his eyes. His brows drew together and she backpedaled in alarm. "Not that…I mean…never mind, just, forget I asked…" her voice trailed away and with a shaking hand, she tried the key again. She jabbed and jabbed at the ignition, unable to sink it.

He reached across and put his hand over hers. She drew back sharply, not wanting another vision like yesterday's. Never wanting to see that again.

"I mean, I've never been here before, on the earth," he says. "I've only ever heard about it."

Kelly shook her head. "How can that be? Aren't you always here, influencing and possessing people or whatever?"

To her surprise, he laughed. His laugh is completely unlike Mark's donkey bray…it is more of a chuckle, throaty and…private is the word that comes strangely to her mind.

"No. That's a big misconception up here. I only punish, I don't make the decisions. There are demons that spend a good deal of time with you—with humans, I mean—influencing people to go wrong…but as far as possession goes…well. In this day and age, I doubt it would even go over at all. They'd probably just be locked up and given thorazine. In the old days, a possession would really throw a scare into people. They just believed more."

He looked over at her, eyebrows up and earnest, looking more like Mark than ever.

She shook her head.

"It's not what we're taught. I always thought that the Devil, that you, spent all your time making people do bad things. Encouraging it, at least."

"No. People have free will. That makes them more than capable of talking themselves into whatever they want to talk themselves into doing. It's one of the things God, Himself and I differed over…one of the reasons I ended up as Hell's attendant."

The car had been getting warmer as the afternoon sun streamed through the windows. Kelly put the key in the ignition, her hands perfectly calm now, and powered down the windows. The fresh breezed felt good on her face. Cool and calming.

The Devil, too, appreciated the breeze. The scents it brought were of food, new buds, and the occasional human that walked by. He could smell exhaust, too, and though it brought with it an inkling of Hell, it was far from the sulfurous stink that was normally his constant.

"So, you know God?" The concept is huge to her, somewhere beyond her comprehension.

"I was an Angel…you were taught that?" he looked at her quizzically.

She nodded assent and for him to go on. But he doesn't. He closed his eyes again but not before she saw the grief cloud his (her brother's) features.

She turned, too, and looked at her hands in her lap. She'd been on the verge of reaching over to him, but had stopped herself. It was only because at certain times he seemed so much Mark…that was the only reason she'd been about to reach out. The thought sparks another.

"How much of him is still in you? Anything?" she asked, not looking up.

He could have thought she meant God. Someone else might have thought it, but the Devil knew who she meant.

"I'm not sure. It would seem an occupied body retains a little bit of 'itself' as far as memories, habits. Especially the really ingrained ones, like cigarettes or drugs," She glanced at him at the mention of drugs, but he wasn't even looking at her. He was looking through his window, face lifted to the breeze. "Amon, one of the demons, said it is a 'taste' of the former occupant, and I think I see what he meant. I have some of your brother's memories, but for rote things, like tying my shoes and knowing what bathrooms are all about," he glanced at her. "We don't have bathrooms in Hell."

She almost smiled, but didn't.

"But how much of Mark is…how much is he aware of?"

The Devil looked at her for a long while, gauging. He laid a hand on hers and in her growing distress, she let him.

"He has no awareness of this, Kelly. His consciousness, his soul, isn't here at all." His hand tightened on hers. "He's in Hell and that's all he knows, now and forever, until God, Himself decrees it otherwise."

Tears slid down her cheeks. She had known this, of course she had. She'd seen him there, after all. But even though she'd seen and even though the Devil had told her this morning when she came after him that there would be no deals, she had still somehow thought…

"What happens when he…when God…decrees otherwise?" Her voice was almost a whisper. "What will happen to Mark then?"

The Devil squeezed her hand again but then let it go.

"Then his soul—all the souls in Hell—will cease to exist." He said it matter-of-factly. Nothing he could say to her would assuage her grief at this.

Kelly bent over the steering wheel and cried. The fear and strangeness of the last four days coupled with the exhaustion she was feeling all bore down at once and broke over her like a wave seeded with lead. She sobbed until her sides and stomach ached, until her throat was raw. She sobbed until the mucous from her nose ran red with blood and the tissues she pulled from her center console were soaked and unusable. She sobbed and a couple walking past behind her car heard but kept walking, the woman thinking how odd it was that the man in the car did nothing to comfort the woman.

Eventually she tapered off and calmed. Her eyes were burning with the salt from her tears and her throat ached and her head...but she felt saner than she'd felt since finding Mark on that rooftop. Since watching him jump.

"I'll take you into Philadelphia, wherever you want to go, but then I'm done," she said. She didn't look at the Devil, didn't see the sorrow in his eyes. "I don't know who you're after and I don't care. I'm sure you have a reason. But I can't be a party to it. Not if it won't help me with my brother."

From the corner of her eye she saw him nod his assent and then movement in her driver's side mirror caught her attention. Something odd. Instinctively, she shifts her gaze to the rearview mirror and she sees a man walking past the back of her car; she could only see from his shoulders down to just below his waist. He was in a plaid flannel and dark blue jeans.

He had a shotgun gripped in one fist.

"Oh my God," she said and twisted to her right to track the man's progress. From the back she can see he has gray hair, slightly bushy, and tan work boots. She couldn't see his face, but the determined set of his shoulders seemed to scream his intent. He was heading to the diner.

"Oh my God, oh my God," Kelly said, fumbling the

phone from her purse. Dead. She pushed the button a few more times, mashing it. "No, oh no, oh my God, oh my God…" She realized she hadn't thought to charge her phone in days.

She looked for the man with the shotgun and saw him just disappearing through the diner's glass front door.

She looked at the Devil. His head was still tilted back against the headrest and his mouth was open. He snored.

She reached out and shook his shoulder. He snorted and snapped awake, looking at her blearily.

"A man just went in the diner with a gun!" she said, her hands gripping themselves at her chest.

He looked over his shoulder at the diner then back at her. He shrugged his shoulders and started to lay his head back against the seat.

"We have to do something! We have to help them!" Her hands ground into each other.

"Do? What do you want to do?"

"He's going to kill someone if we don't do something. My phone is dead, I can't call the police plus it would take too long for them to–" she broke off, mid-sentence, mouth open and staring at the Devil. "You have to do something! You can stop him!"

"Me?" the Devil's eyes widened in surprise. "What would I do? You said he has a gun!"

She stared at him, completely nonplussed.

"Well…you're the Devil, can't you, I don't know…throw a fireball at him or something? Or wait! I know! Show him Hell! Like you showed me. Show him where he's headed! Then he won't do it!"

"No, absolutely not. I'd have to grab onto him to do that and he'd shoot me long before I got the chance to straighten him out." He was shaking his head. "This isn't any of my business. I can't interfere. Let's just get on with–"

"Of course it's your business! That's one of yours that just went in that diner with a shotgun! Maybe a demon coerced him into this…that makes you responsible!"

The Devil shook his head, eyes closed, his face smooth and unconcerned.

"No. Out of the question. I'm not the boss down there, you know. They don't do my bidding or anything. It's not like the stories they tell up here; how many times do I have to tell you?"

In his crossed arm, closed eye posture she saw every selfishness that her brother used to indulge in. The petty, infantile determination to only do what he wanted; when he wanted.

"Well, I'm going in there," she said, opening her door. "You can wait for me or find another way to Philly; that's up to you."

She slammed the door behind her. The Devil opened

his eyes and stared at the ceiling of the car in exasperation. She was being stupid; let her. Let her be as stupid as she wanted. What did he care? He didn't.

He slammed open his car door.

"Kelly! Wait!"

She was crouched behind a car parked in front of the diner. She looked back at him and made an angry shushing gesture. Then she waved her hand for him to come over, but stay low.

"Ridiculous," he said to himself, muttering under his breath as he crouched-walked awkwardly to where she was. Kelly was staring fixedly into the diner, eyes round with frustrated panic. He followed her gaze.

The diner was a small one consisting of booths across the front right under the plate glass windows, and across from the booths, a counter ran the length of the diner with stools bolted to the floor all along it. The kitchen was behind the counter, accessible through two swinging doors.

The man with the gun was standing just to the right of the front door, shotgun at his shoulder and pointing at the waitress who'd just served them. She was standing with her hands fisted together and shoved against her mouth. The man's jaw worked as he talked but Kelly and the Devil couldn't hear him from where they crouched. The man motioned toward the kitchen with the shotgun. The waitress shook her head and pulled her hands away from her mouth, pleading with the man. The gun jerked and he yelled out…something like "you're into it" or "you're trying it"…Kelly couldn't quite make it out. The waitress shook her head and her hands flew apart and fluttered frantically near her shoulders. It was an obvious 'I don't know what you're talking about' gesture.

The man waved the gun again and the waitress screamed but took a step closer to the kitchen. The gun waved again and she screamed again. This time, Kelly could hear her. She'd screamed "No! No Roger!" before taking another sideways step toward the kitchen. The waitress stood just outside the swinging door and when Roger menaced her with the shotgun, she pushed through with a wail they heard in the parking lot.

As soon as Roger had followed the waitress into the kitchen, Kelly broke for the diner's front door. The Devil shook his head and followed her.

Several people lay on the floor, hands over their heads, unaware the shotgun man had gone into the kitchen. Kelly tapped one customer with her foot and he looked up, fear filling his eyes.

"He's gone into the kitchen," she said, more or less mouthing the words, barely audible. "Go outside, call the police."

The man tapped the man next to him and mouthed the same thing and the man tapped the girl nearest him and through this method, the message was passed to every patron. They got up by ones and twos and shuffled quietly to the diner's front door and out, their faces shocked and terrified but also filling with relief.

"Okay, good, you did good," the Devil whispered to Kelly, "Now let's get out of here."

She glanced at him and then back at the kitchen, her lip caught between her teeth. Roger was yelling and the waitress was sobbing and undercutting both of them was another voice; a man's voice, low and conciliatory.

Kelly looked back at the Devil, her green eyes blazing with fear.

"There must be something you can do," she said, breathing the words in a frustrated sigh.

"This isn't any of my business. I'm not going to interfere with the things that go on up here! I'm in enough trouble already, can't you see that?"

"Oh, come on! This isn't part of any divine plan! It's just a loony with a gun! You can do something about it…you're the Devil!" They'd been crouched together behind the counter and now she shoved at his shoulders, urging him up. "Go! Do something!"

He shook his head, but let himself be propelled up. He didn't know why he was letting himself get talked into this. He had to get on with his original mission. Time would run out sooner rather than later, but something about her just compelled him.

"Hey," he said. "Hey, you in there."

There was a sudden silence from the kitchen as if his words had reached in and slapped them all simultaneously.

"Hello?" the Devil said. "Come out, come out, where—"

"Fuck you! Is that the police? Fuck the police!" A rough voice called from the kitchen. The words were muddled and unstable. The Devil could guess who said them. He smiled.

"No, not the police. Just pop on out here and let's get this settled, shall we? I have to be somewhere."

Now the silence from the kitchen had an almost palpable quality of disbelief and it stretched out longer than the first time. Then the same drunken voice called out:

"Uh, hey, Faggot? You might want to get gone. I'm busy right now but I'll be out there in just a second. Hang around if you want your ass handed to you."

The Devil dropped his head and raised his shoulders at Kelly.

"I tried, okay?"

She tilted her head.

"Okay? No it's not okay. Do something."

She made a shooing gesture with her hands.

The Devil sighed and looked up again, addressing the swinging doors:

"Ready or not, here I–"

The doors burst open towards him and the man with the shotgun flew out between them, yelling:

"Okay you asked for it Faggot and now you're–"

The Devil sidestepped and put his foot out and the man went crashing to the floor, landing awkwardly on the gun, breaking his thumb. The waitress and another man were visible through the swinging doors, their mouths open and shocked. Kelly got quick, abbreviated glances of them as the doors swung in smaller and smaller arcs, finally closing on them with a sigh.

The man with the shotgun lay on his stomach, moaning. Kelly started to stand, thinking this was the end of it when the Devil–without looking at her–put his hand near her face, palm up: stay there, don't move. The casual, almost bantering quality he'd had up till now was gone entirely. There was a feeling in the air like that after a lightning strike, ozone and static that makes your stomach tighten in nervousness, and suddenly she wished she hadn't brought him in here. Suddenly he seemed like an extremely dangerous dog that had just slipped his collar.

"Are you all right, darling?" the Devil addressed Roger as he lay moaning on the floor and his voice was low, just on the verge of insinuation and the word that insisted on coursing through Kelly's mind was 'deadly, deadly, deadly' like an unholy mantra. She realized she was not as afraid of the man with the gun on the floor as she was of the man that looked like her brother.

Roger rolled over, intending to surprise the man who'd tripped him, his left hand going to the trigger of the shotgun.

"Fuck you, Faggot–" Roger yelled, pulling the trigger and at the same time squeezing his eyes shut and bracing himself for the kick and roar that would surely follow. But the shotgun didn't kick. And it didn't roar.

Roger squinted his eyes open and the man in the jean jacket stood over him, his chest lined up with the barrels of the gun. His hands were on his hips and he was shaking his head at Roger.

"I thought I knew you," the Devil said. "I knew you seemed familiar in some way. You beat her, right? Just like you used to beat up kids in grade school. You put a little boy in the hospital, I remember. I remember you now." His voice got lower and lower, threaded with a cold menace that made the hair rise on the back of Kelly's neck.

The cook that Roger had accused the waitress of being involved with had taken the opportunity to vamoose through the back door, but the waitress had stayed and now she peered out from between the swinging doors.

Roger glanced at his wife then back to the jean jacket man. His finger still squeezed the trigger.

"Huh?" he said. "No! I don't beat her, I never did! What the hell are you talking about?" Roger now felt some of the same impending doom that had gathered in Kelly's mind. Fear was worming into him and he couldn't understand why. The scrawny faggot in front of him would be no match in a hand to hand, he didn't even need the damn shotgun, what was he scared of? He didn't know. But it didn't serve to lessen his fear; in fact, it only made it worse.

The Devil shook his head at Roger, once left once right.

"Lying? On top of everything else? Not a good idea, Roger. Not good at all."

The Devil placed his index finger at the tip of the shotgun. A tiny, blue flame rolled down the oiled center part of the barrels, splitting them as it went. The barrels peeled apart, curling back on themselves. The flame continued down, the ssshh it made was the loudest sound in the diner.

Kelly's eyes had gone wide and she clasped her hands together at her chest. She was still kneeling and her distressed expression made her look like a penitent at prayer. The spark of blue fire reflected in her eyes, turning the green a murky brown.

Roger watched in stunned amazement as the small ball of flame laid waste to his gun. He couldn't move. His arms were frozen, holding the gun just above his face. Only his left index finger was capable of movement, still squeezing the trigger over and over.

Now the blue flame hit the stock and a wisp of smoke rose behind it as it continued to roll. By now, the split barrels had bent all the way back and imbedded themselves in the floor on either side of Roger's neck, caging his head.

The blue flames left a charred scar down the stock, still smoking, and the smell reminded Kelly of winter and fireplaces and...

The flame hit the end of the stock, which wavered inches from Roger's eyes. It paused, glowing and burning deeper into the hickory wood and then it dropped, hissing, into Roger's left eye.

Kelly screamed and the waitress—who'd been watching from the kitchen—screamed, too, and ran to Roger. She pushed past the Devil and fell to her knees at Roger's side. She wailed and pulled at the gun barrel closest to her as Roger writhed and screamed, shaking his head side to side, bucking and kicking, trying to free himself as the small bit of Hell burned and burned in his eye.

The Devil stepped forward and laid a hand on the waitress's head.

Kelly yelled:

"No! Mark, don't!" Even as the waitress calmed and sat back on her heels, her hands going limp in her lap as she stared vacantly up at the Devil.

From her vantage point behind him, Kelly could only see half the waitress' dazed and wondering face; the rest was blocked by the Devil's khaki-clad leg.

For the waitress, everything disappeared except for the deep green eyes of the jean-jacketed man. Roger and his writhing fell away, the lady behind the counter fell away, the whole diner fell away and she was floating, floating in gray nothing, with only those eyes to guide her. It seemed she floated for hours or days in that murky gray but she wasn't afraid, the eyes stayed with her, she kept looking into the eyes.

A small, blackish lump appeared in her peripheral vision and she wanted to turn to see what it was, but the man's eyes held her. Now the blackish lump was coming closer or she was moving toward it, she couldn't tell which, and the eyes seemed to tell her to get ready, get ready, you will need your strength. But she had no strength, had never had any. It was why she sympathized with Roger, even when he kicked or punched her. She knew that he had a good heart, a good soul; he was just misunderstood. He had no strength. It had been taken from him by the world.

It was the world to blame, not Roger.

The man's voice came to her, floating somehow in the gray, and he asked if she was ready. She said ready for what? And he said to see, are you ready to see?

She said yes I am ready to see. But fear cramped her stomach, squeezing, making her aware she still had a body here in the gray.

Then you will see, the voice said, and she was turning, turning, turned and the black lump was in front of her.

It was slightly larger than a fist and shaped like a human heart, but it was black and dead looking. As she stared, it cracked open down one side and ichor leaked slowly out into the gray, feathering and staining it a dark reddish black. Along with the ichor came a smell…a sick combination of feces and rotting meat. She felt sick to her stomach and afraid. Very afraid.

This is Roger's heart the voice told her and she wanted to protest. She looked at the eyes, wanting to shake her head, no, not my Roger, it isn't, but the eyes were stern, unbending. She looked back at the black heart. Now it spun slowly, pieces of it lifting off and away and hovering steadily. She saw everything: his hate and his self-pity, his vaunting ego, how he despised everyone, everyone, even her. She saw how he despised her. And it broke her heart.

He will be mine in Hell, the voice said, and it is right that it should be so. Do you see that?

She nodded. It is right, she thought, and now she cried.

Do you, also, want to be mine in Hell? the voice said.

And she was very afraid. She'd been raised Catholic but hadn't given it much thought since about tenth grade, but now she felt her mortal soul within her, felt it with all the certainty of an eighty-year-old priest on his death bed.

No, she said, the tears heavier.

Then you should not journey his path with him. The choice is yours, the voice said and all at once, she was back in the diner.

The lady behind the counter was yelling:

"No! Mark, don't!"

Roger writhed and writhed, screaming.

The waitress stood, brushing the hem of her uniform down. She glanced once at the man in the jean jacket then she turned and walked out the front door.

Sirens in the distance forced Kelly up and onto her feet.

"We have to get out of here," she said, taking the Devil's hand.

She started toward the swinging doors but he stopped her, his hand gripping hers. She turned back to him, suddenly shy to look into his face. Her eyes met his. She nodded.

He looked into her eyes, searching, and then nodded back.

They pushed through the swinging doors and into the kitchen.

The back door was still open, swinging a bit.

Kelly and the Devil passed through and into the bright sunlight of early afternoon.

* * *

She drove smoothly and competently, even though her nerves were singing. She felt like a high-tension wire, taut and alive with electrical current, dangerous, maybe deadly. She saw Roger in her mind, his writhing, bucking dance played over and over, and each slam of his booted feet seemed to say your fault, your fault, you brought this demon in upon me. Though some part of her wanted to see this as a burden of guilt, she found a larger part of her accepted the responsibility without regret. She'd brought the Devil into the diner, yes, but Roger had brought everything else upon himself. He had only himself to blame.

Outwardly her features did not change, but inside she smiled. Not a smile of triumph, not one of satisfaction or even righteousness, the smile was one of acceptance. She had accepted her own responsibility and found she could hoist the weight. Easily.

She glanced at the Devil next to her and for the first

time, she saw him as wholly another, an entity apart from Mark, not her brother. She was awed by him, her mysterious passenger, and drawn to him. Not in the way you'd be drawn to an attractive stranger across a room, but in the way you are drawn to watch a thunderstorm, magnetized and frightened at the same time, unable to turn away from the firework display.

The Devil considered her feelings as she felt them. He couldn't read her mind as such, but having made a bond with her by showing her Hell, he had a good idea of at least the flavor of her thoughts. And he was troubled.

He felt drawn to her, too, to her innate goodness and the strength that was her base, her basic nature. In the topography of Kelly, her bedrock was pure iron. There was something of an Angel's character in her combination of strength and kindness, a balance, and it was beautiful. There was no beauty in Hell, and he found that in having it, he would miss it more when he had to return.

It had been a very long time since he'd been in Heaven and this woman next to him reminded him of that sad fact. And yet at the same time, her presence assuaged his grief.

He was very troubled.

They had stopped twice more for food and the Devil had eaten prodigiously each time. He could feel this body around him like a vehicle and it thrummed and revved, souped up and developing quickly, its metabolism almost literally on fire. Torn muscle rebuilt itself, gobbling the protein the Devil ingested. Tendons began to loosen, oiled by the physical activity he was putting this body through. And all the while, the clamoring for drugs faded and faded, becoming wee, winking out.

They were on the bridge to Philadelphia and the sun was hanging at the horizon as though too curious about the state of this part of the world to sink the rest of the way down. Kelly flicked on her lights as they curved onto the Vine Street Expressway, merging with the traffic.

"Just anywhere in Center City?" she said. "Are you sure?"

The Devil nodded, knowing she could see his profile, at least peripherally. He had disengaged from her thoughts/feelings/being and was concentrating on his mission. He kept Thomas Evigan in the forefront of his mind and began to quest.

"Listen," Kelly said, exiting the sunken expressway and emerging into almost full dark. They were in the city now and she piloted the car absently, heading to Market Street and the middle of downtown. "I can stay and help while you search. You might need a driver, someone to help you get around." She glanced at him again. He was very still, looking out the front windshield, but, she got the feeling, seeing nothing. In the past half hour, she'd felt an almost physical lessening of him, as though he was taking himself away even as he sat next to her.

"What do you think?" she asked. "Do you want me to stay?"

He looked at her then, his eyes clearing as though coming awake from a dream. He tilted his head like he was surprised to see her.

"Stay? No." he said, and turned from her. "This is not for you to be a part of."

"Why?" she asked, the hurt evident in her voice. "All I want to do is—"

He shook his head. Once left, once right and she was reminded of him using that gesture with Roger.

She pulled into an alley off Market and pulled to the side, where service vehicles parked.

"I just want to help," she said and though she was afraid, she put a hand on his arm.

He turned to her again and she saw a brief flash in his eyes, not of anger but of something that made her unsure…was it sadness she saw?

"Kelly, you'd be putting your mortal soul in jeopardy. I can't let you."

Another thrill of fear coursed through her and she felt her soul like a vulnerable, living thing inside her that required protection. She nodded.

"Okay, I understand, but…" she blushed and he could

not see it, it was too dark where they sat, but he knew it anyway. "Call me then, I guess, if there's anything I can do. If you need a ride or anything."

He felt her smile, small and sad. And it tore into him. He put his hand on his door handle, almost as if, in self-defense of his feelings, he'd need to make a fast escape from the car.

"No," he said. "I won't call. You're out of this. I shouldn't have asked even as much as I have. I shouldn't have involved you to this degree. I...I regret–"

At his words, she'd felt herself growing sadder, but when he said that he regretted her, her head snapped back in surprised misunderstanding.

"You regret it?" she said, hurt threading her voice.

He reached for her hand.

"I don't regret you, that's not what I–"

Kelly had turned to face him, twisted with her back to the window. Even as he reached forward, conciliatory, her door burst open behind her, bending in a screech of tearing metal, all the way back to the front tire.

Kelly was pulled out into the night.

In one smooth motion, the Devil grasped his own door handle, depressed it and rolled from the car. He landed on the balls of his feet and forcing this body beyond its abilities, he sprang up and onto the roof. He reached up and his hand grazed the underside of Kelly's shoe as she was pulled into the sky.

An eerie, shrieking laugh split the night air and echoed back and forth between the building walls. Kelly continued to rise, struggling, reaching for him, her face a frozen, white, fearful mask. At the level of the fifth story, a balcony jutted out into the dark. Kelly was flipped up and over onto the balcony, disappearing from the Devil's sight.

Standing on the balcony's stone railing was another demon.

The Devil stared up, making his own face a mask. Then he waved.

"Hello Lillith," he said. "It's nice to see you again."

Lillith, the demon on the balcony, had not been expecting this response. Her features drew together in irritation. She'd commandeered a whore's body and the face was still beautiful if a little pinched; witchy and hungry.

Suits her, the Devil thought.

"That one suits you, Lillith," he called up.

Surprise raced across her features, then pleasure followed quickly by suspicious anger.

"What do you mean by that? Suits me?" she said, calling down. She'd jumped lightly to the surface of the balcony and held Kelly's head pinned between her knees, Kelly's back against the wall. Kelly struggled but the demon's body was strong of leg and held her easily.

"It's obviously a body that's had more than a few rough miles," he said. "It's fitting that its last miles should be over the roughest road imaginable. Meaning, my dear, that you are, shall we say, tough to contain."

Pleasure and anger flitted across her features again. She didn't know if she was being insulted or not, but she suspected that she was.

She squeezed her legs together and Kelly moaned in pain. Her head felt as though it was in a vise. There was very little in the way of padding on the whore's wretched knees.

The Devil controlled his features, not wanting Lillith to see his distress. Although he imagined she could sense it. That was Lillith's way–she was a Seer of all things.

"Yes, I do know how you feel about this one," Lillith said and pinched again. Kelly yelped this time as the knees ground against her temples. Now Lillith smiled down. "Who would have guessed it? Lucifer loses his mind…for the second time, too!" Her voice became lilting, teasing. "I wouldn't have thought you'd forget your lesson so soon, Lucifer. It was such a hard lesson to learn." She shook her head, her smile growing wider. "Ever miss Heaven? Or are you over that now?"

The Devil smiled back. He knew he walked a fine line. He wanted to goad her into coming down but he was also causing Kelly more distress. He would have to count on Kelly's strength. He had no choice.

"I wonder if you miss it, Lillith," he said. "Or do you think earth is more your style?"

Lillith squeezed Kelly's head again and then let go entirely, jumping up and over the balcony railing. Tearing fingernails from their beds, she climbed down, hand over hand, clinging to the wall like a bat.

The Devil kept his face neutral. Kelly's head appeared over the balcony edge and she looked shaken but okay. He shifted all his attention to the descending demon.

She hit the ground and turned so fast she was nearly a blur. She was on him in a second. She wrapped herself around him, an arm around his neck, another around his waist and one long leg coming around his hips. She tightened like a constrictor and smiled into his eyes.

"What do you think of this body, now, Lucifer," she said, breathing the words into his ear, drawing out the ess in his name.

He felt this body responding, growing hard against her pelvis. Autonomic response, he thought to himself. That's all it is.

Sensing his thought, she pulled back, a pout on her fleshy lips. Her eyes were darkly rimmed and the pupils glittered eerily from the depths of her eyes.

"Let's not kid each other, Lucifer; you miss heaven as much as I, and we always will miss it." Her voice lost its teasing note, displaying the truth of her statement.

"It's true, Lillith, I do miss it," he said, putting his hands on her shoulders, stepping back and disentangling himself. "So, what's your plan, my dear? How were you going to get me to go back?"

She looked up at him and smiled. She reached into her short, leather jacket and withdrew a knife that looked too big to have been concealed in that tight space. She smiled at his expression of mild surprise.

"Nice, isn't it?" Without further hesitation, she thrust herself forward, grabbing his wrist in one hand, knife out and questing. The Devil turned, but not before the knife caught the trailing edge of his jacket, slicing through. Lillith turned almost as fast, her nails digging into the flesh of the Devil's borrowed wrist, drawing blood.

He shook his hand, trying to dislodge her, but she held firm. She struck out again and he ducked and spun on his heels, drawing her arm up and over his head. He stood and snapped her against himself, the knife pinned between them.

He looked into her eyes, not smiling. He couldn't let her go to make a grab for the knife; she was too strong. Without forethought, he brought his forehead sharply into hers, a sick, cracking noise filling his head. She staggered back, dazed, head split across the middle like a seam and he reached for the knife. She brought it up, slicing across the meat of his palm, and still her other hand held his wrist. It was as if they were welded together at the join.

He grabbed her flailing knife hand and she thrust her head forward, her lips seeking his neck, his jugular. He could not let her latch onto him there. It would be the end of him.

He ran his knee up and into her stomach and she heaved out breath, stumbling back, finally dropping the knife. He took the opportunity and grabbed her thin throat with his free hand and squeezed. He was careful not to squeeze the life right out of her…with her hand on his arm, he'd be dragged back to Hell with her, and that was not in his plan.

He leaned forward and propelled her, titling and stumbling, to the alley wall. "Time for you to go, Lillith," he said, his voice harsh and panting. Holding her was like trying to hold a deadly, twining python. "You don't have to go home," he said and slammed her bodily into the brick wall for emphasis, "but you can't stay here." Slam.

Her eyes slitted in amusement and laughter tried to squeeze through the narrowed opening of her throat. Then she brought her own knee up.

It landed squarely in the Devil's groin and he felt first a sharp pain, but nothing that would make him lose his grip. Then came a wave of nausea as a sickening heat radiated through his groin and up into his lower belly. The pain continued to radiate even as the nausea built.

Lillith pulled herself up and away from his collapsing form and she ascended the wall the way she'd come down, hand over hand, animal-like. She reached the balcony and flipped herself up and over. Kelly was gone. Lillith shrieked in frustrated rage. The woman was her one bargaining chip…she had to find her before Lucifer did.

The balcony was small, merely a decorative outcrop on the façade of the building. The window that faced it was one solid sheet of glass, not intended to open. Lillith looked up but it was a sheer face to the next balcony. The woman could not have climbed it. She looked left to the fire escape that snaked up the side of the building. It was easily ten feet away…the woman could not have bridged that gap. Then Lillith looked down, examining the side of the building. There was the barest suggestion of a ledge, a mere three inches of extended brick, but if the woman had been very brave, very strong, she might have done it.

Lillith leapt from the balcony and flung herself against the wall. Gripping with the whore's already shredded fingers, forcing this body to work well beyond its limits, she crabbed across the building and onto the fire escape.

Up or down? She hadn't gone down; she'd be by Lucifer's side if she had. She must have gone up. Lillith began to climb the fire escape stairs. She went quietly on the toes of her feet, listening behind her for Lucifer. He would recover himself quickly. Perhaps had already. She gained the roof.

Kelly was mid-way across the grainy surface, struggling with a door that would lead into the building. She'd heard the struggle between the Devil and the woman (demon? Had to be, yes) and after considering her very limited options, had clambered across to the fire escape. It had been a terrifying, tenuous trek as she'd listened to the brutal exchange in the alley below her.

Now she turned at a light scraping sound behind her. The woman (demon) was coming over the fire-escape and onto the roof. The woman-demon's face was slicked red from the gash in her forehead. The blood had run down her neck, soaking the cheap blouse she wore, blooming black roses in the rayon. Her hands, before they clenched into fists, displayed ragged fingertips, ground down nearly to the bone.

Kelly's stomach seemed to slam up and into her throat and for a moment, she was unable to breathe. Terror froze her where she stood, even as the woman-demon gritted across the roof to her. She was smiling, her teeth the brightest thing in that mask of blood. She was horrific.

Kelly's legs lost what little strength they had left and she slid down, sighing, her back to the door. The demon's smile grew wider.

"No fight left in you, little lamb?" the demon said, her voice cracking and throaty from the Devil's handiwork at her throat. Kelly's stomach tightened again and her heart stuttered in her chest, making her gasp.

Now the demon was upon her and Kelly could only stare up, transfixed by the nightmare before her. The body the demon piloted looked half dead, beaten and tattered, ill-used. A swell of pity caused tears to form in Kelly's eyes. Pity that someone could have used her only body, her only life, so uncaringly but worse to have that body end up as a demon's mode of transport…to be used up and discarded as easily as you'd discard a sock with a hole…

Lillith felt the pity and took a step back, suddenly unsure. Then she knelt, puzzled and staring at the woman. There was something…something…curious…

"Who are you?" Lillith whispered, her eyes slitting suspiciously. She shook her head like a dog bothered by a fly.

Kelly pushed herself more firmly against the door and turned her head as the demon reached toward her with shattered, shaking fingers. Kelly barely registered the demon's question, so great was her fear. She would remember the question, but only later.

The demon's fingers traced her cheek.

"Lillith, leave her alone," the Devil said, standing fifteen feet away at the edge of the roof. "Turn and fight. Let's have done with it."

Lillith turned and rose in one fluid movement. Dazed incomprehension shuttered her features, but from the distance the Devil could not see it.

Lillith started toward him. "Lucifer, you must—"

She stumbled and went to her knees, head down. This body was almost done in, but it was more than that that made her stumble…it was what she'd seen in the woman…

She got to her feet and stumbled forward again, forcing the legs into a run. She must tell Lucifer what she'd seen. Her ankle snapped and she felt the pain as something distant, of no consequence. She forced the body up again.

The Devil stood his ground, letting Lillith come closer. He wanted her as far from Kelly as her could get her. Lillith was wholly untrustworthy and more than capable of killing Kelly for her own purposes. He didn't see the demon's alarm in the whore's face—its mask of blood hid every feature save the bright, staring eyes.

"Lucifer, listen," Lillith said, her voice an incomprehensible, blood-filled buzz. "You must watch out, you must watch out for her, she's—"

She was upon him, stumbling, arms outstretched, her mouth a wide grimace. The Devil took her arms and side-stepped, using her own momentum against her and flinging her from the roof. Lillith tried to grip onto Lucifer's arms, but the fingers of this body were slick with blood and frozen by fatigue.

She couldn't do it.

She fell.

Lucifer watched until the body hit, bursting like an overripe fruit, then turned and strode across the roof to Kelly.

By the time they got back to the alley, Lillith's Transition was almost complete. She stood near their car, the headlights of cars passing on the street illuminating what little was left of her. She was almost entirely faded. At the sight of Kelly, she tilted her head as though listening.

Kelly was startled by the almost-not-there apparition.

"How long will she be like that?" Kelly asked.

The Devil looked at Lillith, his face an odd combination of sad and stern.

"It can take a while. The Transition is…it's difficult. And she'll be remanded to Hell for a while this time. They can interfere up here, but they can't outright try and kill humans. Very frowned upon."

Kelly couldn't take her eyes from Lillith. She still appeared in the body she'd chosen, but now it wasn't as beaten as it had been toward the end. Kelly glanced at the body that had fallen from the roof and quickly away, the pity swelling through her again.

"For killing this person, you mean?" she gestured to the ruin on the ground half way down the alley.

"No, that person was already dying as Lillith took her over, it's the only way. I mean you. For trying to kill you; for even implying it."

Kelly shook her head.

"She didn't try to kill me."

The Devil glanced at Lillith, startled. She was looking at him intently, trying to convey something. Her lips moved, but no sound emerged, she'd gone too far to the other side.

"What do you mean?" the Devil said.

"At the end, I didn't get the feeling she was trying to kill me. She scared me, badly, but…she had plenty of time, if killing me had been her plan…" Kelly trailed off, looking at Lillith, remembering her trembling fingers as they slid gently down her cheek. "She could have killed me. She didn't."

The Devil looked at Lillith again. She was almost gone, but the Devil could see she'd gone beyond the point of caring about this world. Her face was full of lost, desperate fear…she was Transitioning.

As they stood watching, the demon faded until she was barely a glimmer in the dark and then she faded into nothingness.

* * *

Tremors coursed through Kelly's body as she sat behind the wheel. She stretched her arms out and grasped the steering wheel trying to steel her limbs against the shakes, but they came again, swelling through her, making her teeth chatter. Delayed reaction. That's what this was. Her body trying to rid itself of that excess adrenalin. That's all it was.

The Devil stood next to her window, bent over, his arms resting on the ledge. He didn't want her to go, but more than that, he didn't want her in jeopardy. This had gotten so complicated, so quickly. How had that happened? Is that what it's like, being human?

He looked at her profile. Her eyes were closed and her hair was tucked behind her ear. She looked noble from the side, strong-featured; a face you'd see in a painting.

"If you really want me to go, then I will," she said, still not opening her eyes. Her hands tightened even more on the steering wheel.

The Devil nodded. He wanted her to go and didn't want her to go. But he wouldn't put her in jeopardy again for his own selfishness.

He leaned in and kissed her lightly on the cheek. Then he stood and turned and started down the alley. He felt overwhelmingly as though he were abandoning her. Everything in him sung out, calling him to return to her, be near her, protect her. But he knew it was just selfishness and perhaps a bit of the man who'd been her brother. Some bit of Mark wanting to look out for his sister.

The Devil set his shoulders and turned out onto Market Street. There was almost no traffic. The sky above him glimmered on the verge of first light. He could see the breath this body generated and he closed his jacket.

Then he started toward mid-town. He marveled at the ache in his chest. All his time in Hell had never once produced this living, grieving pain. Had he done the wrong thing by sending her away? His heart told him that he had.

He turned and trotted back the way he'd come. He turned into the alley, on the verge of calling her name, but the syllables died on his outward breath.

She was gone.

* * *

Kelly drove the two hours home, her mind reeling. She

kept the radio on and sang, belting out one song after another, sometimes crying, ignoring her exhaustion and confusion. She was determined to propel herself forward and to forget…everything.

At home, she stripped and showered, leaving her dirty clothes in a bundle on the bathroom floor. She floated her favorite nightgown over her head and down over her body and sank into bed. Thoughts tried to force themselves upon her, but she cleared her mind, allowing exhaustion to do its job and she drifted.

She tried to pin her mind to every day things, trying to clear the fog of the last five confused days. She had to check the bills, call the neighbor to see if she wanted to split the cost of flowers, contact the lawn service, and come up with something to tell work about why she'd called out for the last week.

Thomas was a good boss, if somewhat opaque, but as the owner of Evigan and Partners, he expected a lot from everyone in his employ, even his secretary.

* * *

Kelly drove into Princeton and to the law firm of Evigan and Partners. The office was right off Nassau street and this early in the morning, just after six-thirty, there was very little traffic. Thomas liked her to be in first, open the office, set up coffee and arrange for a delivery of bagels from the small deli down the street. She handled everything, but was too conscious of the dark circles under her eyes and the stuffed feeling of her head.

She thought too, about what she would tell Thomas when he questioned her on her 'family emergency'. She couldn't very well tell him her brother had died; she couldn't tell anyone. There was no body, no funeral, and no official certificate of his death.

That thought led her to what would happen when the Devil had finished his work here on earth. He would leave the body behind, just as that other demon had left the whore's body behind after it had fallen; after it had served its purpose. The thought made her angry and sad, neither emotion lasting long in her exhausted state.

She arranged the warm bagels into two baskets, her hands shaking. Tears tightened the back of her throat and refracted her sight, but she refused to let them fall. She hoped for a busy day filled with phone calls and appointments. So she wouldn't have to keep thinking.

* * *

How much time had passed on Earth as the Devil lay below, unquiet in his sleep, tortured by the death of little Brian? Five years. Five years had passed since the woman-child that killed Brian had won her freedom with the help of Thomas Evigan. Five years that Thomas Evigan had reaped the benefits of swarming media coverage. Five years where he'd watched the tide change as drinks and dinners were bought for him and sycophants came in droves to celebrate the opening of his practice.

Five years on Earth are as nothing for the Devil who has been in Hell almost since before time existed. Our time on Earth is a frantic swirl amounting to very little compared to the sentence set down by God, Himself on Lucifer.

Kelly had almost no recollection of the Carrie Walsh case. Five years ago, Kelly had been twenty-three, only one year older than the woman on trial for killing her own son. Kelly hadn't watched or read any news in that time and in fact had not really been aware of much that was going on in the world…because Kelly had been in a fight for her own life.

She'd been a junior at Rutgers, New Brunswick when the accident happened. She was older than the average junior because her time—and most of her parents' resources—had gone to helping Mark. Between one thing and another, she'd started college two years later than she'd intended.

It was late at night and she and four friends were walking home from a party, giggling and shushing each other, pushing playfully and giggling more. They were on their street, the tall, brick row houses mostly taken over by students, and they were less than a block from home. It had been chilly but not yet cold; the street was wet with a late fall rain that had flattened the layers of orange and yellow leaves blown down over the last three days.

The pickup truck had seemed to come from the very darkness itself, swerving back and forth from lane to lane, no lights on and moving very fast. Kelly's girlfriend, Angie, had seen it first.

"Oh my God, look at this drunk asshole," she'd said, shaking her head and wrapping her scarf more tightly around her neck.

Two of the others had turned to look, but Kelly and another girl, Chrissy, had caught each other up in a clumsy waltz and they were humming as they spun and hopped around the other three girls. Kelly never heard Angie.

As the truck drew closer, Angie had an uneasy thought that it could slide right off the street and hit them. She glanced at the flattened, soggy leaves in the road and then back to the truck.

"Girls, we better– "

At that moment, the truck's lights came on, pinning Angie and the others in their glare, skidding across the lanes, coming right for them. Angie put her hands up, arms straight out and locked in panic. She screamed. Kelly and Chrissy's romp came to a jerking halt as Kelly saw Angie's face, illuminated in the headlights. Kelly didn't even get a chance to turn around before the truck was upon them.

The truck slid sideways, lights flashing away from the huddled group of girls. It bounced when it hit the curb, but it was a low curb and the truck was going very fast when it hit and it did not deter it in the least. The truck gained the sidewalk and ran into the girls broadside. Kelly felt herself pushed roughly forward into Angie. Her vision was filled with Angie's eyes, so large they seemed to take up her whole face. Angie's mouth was a cavern that Kelly felt she was falling into, falling as the truck continued around, pushing the girls down, the tires catching Angie's feet and legs. She and the two other girls were pulled beneath the truck even as Kelly was pushed up and over by the force, almost as though Angie's body were a wave she was riding. Chrissy was crushed as the bed of the truck plowed into the town house behind them and Kelly was thrown fifteen feet, her head connecting with the porch railing. She rebounded neatly into the bed of the truck where it had finally come to rest against the base of the porch.

From where she lay, she heard the driver's side door open, felt the truck lean and rebound as the driver exited, and then came the sound of pounding footsteps disappearing into the night. Lights were coming on up and down the street. She saw the sky above her, black and thick with stars. So many stars, had there always been that many? They were beautiful…

Voices surrounded her, screams, and then a siren. Where was Angie? And Chrissy? Were her friends all right? She wanted to ask someone but she found she couldn't move. She was just tired. So tired. She didn't want to close her eyes. She stared up, blinking, tears running coldly down her cheeks. She could feel the tears. But she couldn't feel anything else. She closed her eyes. I just need to rest a minute.

She opened her eyes in the ambulance. An attendant smiled down at her.

"We're almost there, you're okay," he said. His eyes were blue, sky blue, shining. She found that she loved him. She tried to tell him so.

"Don't try to talk, you have a tube in your throat," he said, reaching over her and out of her sightline, adjusting something. "You were very lucky. You might not think so right away, but…it's amazing you survived that. Really unbelievable." He shook his head. Kelly felt a pit form in her stomach.

My friends, she wanted to ask, are they okay?

The attendant smiled again.

"Someone was looking out for you," he said and his eyes seemed to change, getting darker, cobalt, deep ocean, soothing. She floated.

Then she floated away.

She floated for another month while she healed. She had two broken collar bones, a laceration across the top of her head that almost left her scalped (in the Doctor's mysteriously nauseating words: 'partially degloved'), a ruptured spleen, three broken fingers and a very serious spinal cord injury. It was the spinal cord injury that caused her the year of fighting for an upright position and several painful surgeries that had left the scars on her neck. The year that Carrie Walsh went on trial with Thomas Evigan at her side.

Kelly had not been able to rejoin her graduating class at Rutgers. After her recovery, she'd gotten the secretarial job at the Evigan and Partners law firm because the early hours allowed her the time at night to try and finish her degree.

Kelly had mild twinges of anxiety from time to time, anxious to get it done, but life with her brother had taught her how to temper her impatience.

Now she stepped back, double-checking that the coffee was brewing and everything was ready for the day, knowing Thomas would be the first one in after her; he always was. Kelly admired his dedication.

She went to her desk in reception—really just the foyer of the old house that had been converted to office space. Kelly liked being tucked over to the side under the stained glass window. There was a row of three chairs opposite her, their backs against the stairs, but there was rarely anyone to sit there. Clients were generally greeted within seconds of Kelly informing someone that they were there. It gave the whole practice a very warm, very homey feel.

Thomas Evigan was very aware of that, even as he drove to the small lot behind his building. It used to be where a detached, three-car garage sat, but it had been torn down to make room for more cars. Thomas didn't even have his name on his parking space; none of the parking was reserved except for four spots that had discreet 'guest parking' signs on them.

He exited his Audi, grabbing his attaché case (empty) and stood for a minute looking up at his building. It was a Victorian that had probably once housed a professor and his family. Princeton was a stone's throw away.

Thomas liked that it was residential looking as opposed to a modern office building. He recognized that this house worked two ways: rich clients saw it as old money charming while poor clients (sometimes his most lucrative in the long run) tended to see the crumbling porch floorboards and the woodwork softened by the thick coats of sometimes peeling paint and they were not intimidated.

He also knew it gave him a hometown advantage as it put him in the midst of the people he knew he'd someday govern. He got involved with the locals and local government, mostly through charity work, careful to ruffle as few feathers as necessary for his climb. He'd already been voted onto the Town's Board of Selectmen and he knew that it was just the beginning of his rise. Mayor would not be that far off and after that, well…on his best days, even the presidency of the United States did not seem out of his grasp.

To be fully trusted, he'd have to take a wife, and very soon, because children were part of the equation, too. The problem was finding a woman who'd understand the life she was signing on for. He had no intention of being faithful or of being too much involved in the day-to-day raising of children. That's what wives—and when he was rich enough, nannies—were responsible for.

Thinking about his future wife, he entered the office. Kelly was at the reception desk. She smiled and stood to take his jacket. She looked nervous and he wondered why.

He'd hired her because she was smart and she was plain. She wouldn't cause any trouble for him with the other lawyers or their wives. Thomas only hired male lawyers, and was determined that no office romance would sully the reputation of his firm. At least not until it was big enough to easily digest that type of scandal.

He had difficulty looking at Kelly. To him, her plainness was almost rude in its unrelenting forthrightness, but at least she dressed nicely. When he was a bit more successful, either this year or next, he'd let her go and hire some eye candy.

"Good morning, Kelly," he said and smiled. Then, remembering that she hadn't been in for five days, he tightened his features in concern. "I hope everything is all right. We've really missed you." In fact, he'd barely noticed her absence except as a mild annoyance when he entered or exited the building. "And we've missed the bagels! Did you have them delivered this morning?"

He'd turned away to sort through a small stack of mail and was unaware of the mild flash of hurt in her eyes. He turned back, smiling wider.

"Hmm? Did you say something?" he asked.

"No, I…I didn't," Kelly said, recovering. "Thank you, it's good to be back. If we could talk at some point later, I'd like to explain…it was a family emergency, and–"

"No need!" he flicked a hand at her, cutting her off. "I'm just happy you're back with us, safe and sound." He smiled wider and then turned away down the hall.

"Thank…thank you, I appreciate–"

He turned back again, cutting her off. Now there was concern on his face. Kelly tensed, anticipating a question about the 'emergency' or a commiseration at the very least.

"Were you able to get the bagels?"

* * *

Thomas tilted back in his office chair and enjoyed the dry, toasted bagel. This was the only carb he allowed himself. Let the other politicians get fat; he'd do P90X and eat mostly protein and then let's see who wins at the beauty contest of life.

He finished and let his feet fall, feeling his mind revving and lunging, ready to chew up the day ahead. He woke his computer and went first to email. He was happy to see at least five emails related to his newly created blog. He had a PR agency ghostwrite it for him. He wasn't worried about the agency letting it slip that he wasn't the author of his posts; the owner himself, Sal, did the writing and Thomas had him on a very short leash. He knew exactly where his skeletons were.

Sometimes Thomas thought that was one of the best things about being a lawyer…the leverage it generated.

He opened the email alerts to comments on his blog and his mood soured. That little cunt was still at it. Would she ever get the hint and back the fuck off?

She'd posted three of the five comments:

[Evigan Partners] New Comment on: Taxed by Taxes. User Carrie Walsh commented: OMG Thomas, you are sooooo rite! My paretns pay taxes and they are all ways complaining!

[Evigan Partners] New Comment on: Safer Streets. User Carrie Walsh commented: Were I live its mexicans that r making it sooo unsafe for every 1 espeshilly girls like me! ;)

[Evigan Partners] New Comment on: Safer Streets. User Carrie Walsh commented: Mexicnas should be shipped back 2 costa rico or wear ever they are coming from! Leave us 'pretty girlz' alonnnne!!!1!! ;)

Thomas sighed and logged into his blog and systematically deleted her posts, his face set in grim lines of barely controlled fury. He hoped no one had seen them. He would talk to Sal, the owner of the PR firm, about setting up a system that would send Sal alerts every time a comment got posted so that he could check them and take them down immediately, if required.

He'd also have to do something about Carrie, but it wouldn't be easy. Thomas knew her childish, semi-literate jabberings were actually a carefully conceived cover for her intelligence and brutally cold nature. In his opinion, Carrie was a psychopath, but by now, he'd almost forgotten the amount of fear she drove into him.

He'd briefly considered banging her after the trial was over. She had a certain trailer park babe attractiveness that drew him, but thank God, he'd never acted on it. He couldn't imagine how clingy—or possibly deadly—she'd have been if he had.

He'd have to contact her, take her out and try to make her see reason. He couldn't have her dogging him around for the rest of his career. She was too much bad luck and too many bad vibes in one scary little package.

* * *

The Devil stood on the 600 block of Market Street and considered his options. Traffic was very thick and the city had already developed a pissy smell, though the spring day was mild. It seemed to blow primarily from the subway tunnel yawning before him. The smells and sounds, the anonymous and aggressive pedestrians, all gave him a sense of being back in Hell. It made him very uneasy.

On top of that was the nagging certainty that he should not have left Kelly.

He had two addresses in his pocket—one for Carrie Walsh and one for Thomas Evigan, but the Evigan address, at least, was out of date. He couldn't be sure of the Carrie Walsh one. The clerk he'd talked to hadn't any idea where Thomas Evigan had gone after leaving his Philly practice in the blaze of Walsh-case-victory glory.

"I heard he went somewheres out near Trenton, maybe, somewhere like that. Central Jersey, who knows? On to bigger and better things, I guess. Guy was kind of a dick, really. But I guess that's how you make it big around here."

The clerk was heavy-set and glum. He'd just learned that his job was being terminated at the end of the month. Money was tight in Philly and times were tough and maybe he shoulda stuck with his first idea to drive one of the city busses. Oh well, too late for that, now. He'd sighed, looking at the skinny junkie at his window. Guy wanted that scumbag Evigan's address? Let him have it! Probably this guy was a former client of his anyway. He wants that baby-killers address? No problem! He looks like trouble and that cold-hearted bitch could use some trouble...deserved it, really, for what she'd done.

"They're supposta send it in if they changed their address and there's no change form in her file. Course, lots of 'em don't bother. Guess they don't care to see what the courts have to send 'em."

Carrie had been put on probation, a condition of being found guilty of endangering the welfare of a child–the only thing the jury had found her responsible for. That probationary period had lasted four years. She might have gone anywhere in the last year.

But, the Devil decided, it was a better lead than the address for Evigan. He'd find Carrie and see if he could track Evigan down through her.

He turned and descended the subway's concrete steps. It was dank in the tunnel; the air as stale and fetid as that in a mausoleum. The people waiting on the platform were washed out by the grayish-yellow glow of the tunnel overheads. They stood, mute and still, like stunned cattle, their eyes deep black sockets in their heads. They looked like the forerunners for an army of the dead.

A snake of unease slid up the Devil's spine as his feet hit the platform. He scanned the huddled forms lined up before him. Something was not right here. His mind went, unbidden, to Kelly. The space before him became indistinct, unimportant. He ruminated on his love for her, for that's what it was: love.

Then he shook his head, realizing.

"Hello, Sitri," he said, and waited for the demon to reveal himself.

Two of the huddled forms on the platform stepped apart. Sitri stepped between them and stamped his foot, one hand on his hip, the other twisted into the air in a 'ta-da' gesture. He was a very powerful demon and his presence alone could strengthen interest into blinding, deadly obsession. That's why he'd thought so strongly about Kelly.

The body Sitri occupied was that of an older man in his seventies. He had theatrically flowing white hair and the eyes in his seamed face were a cold blue-gray. The body was tall and trim and moved with the gracefulness of a much younger man.

The Devil nodded in acknowledgement.

"Hello, Sitri," he said. "I must say that I am surprised to see you."

The demon smiled widely, breaking his borrowed face into deep fissures, the wrinkles folding in upon themselves like a gravity defying mudslide.

"Lucifer, old friend," Sitri said and stepped one small step, sliding a foot forward along the concrete and clicking his heels sharply together…ssss, click! "I've been hearing odd tales from down below." He glanced at the nails on his right hand and took another small step closer…ssss, click. "Very odd, indeed." He dipped long, white fingers into the inside pocket of the sport coat he wore and extracted a brown cigarette even more slender than his fingers…ssss, click.

"Stand where you are, Sitri; come no closer," the Devil's voice dropped, becoming soft and sinuous, twined with steel tendrils of warning. If Kelly were present, the feeling of impending danger would have slid once again into her mind. The crowd at the platform shuffled and uneasy moans broke from several mouths. Then they were still.

Sitri looked up, eyebrows raised as he fished a lighter from his front pants pocket. He tilted his head to light the cigarette, his eyes never leaving the Devil. Fresh smoke drew a curtain over his features and then cleared. Sitri was smiling, the cigarette clamped in his teeth.

"Lucifer, what's the trouble? Afraid I've come to collect you?" he said and spread his arms wide, palms up.

The eyes of Mark's body were fixed and heavy lidded. The Devil had become still but taut; slow, deep breaths expanded Mark's chest. He curled his hands into loose fists and bent slightly forward. His eyes never left the demon before him.

"Come on, then," the Devil said, now his voice all menace but undercut by an eagerness that would have stopped a mortal's heart. "Let's get this over with."

Sitri threw his head back and laughed, hands on his hips. The laugh was full and throaty, but the Devil heard the thread of unease tied up in it.

"Lucifer, please!" Sitri said, wiping tears from his eyes. He chuckled and shook his head. "Look at you! So ready to fight! My goodness, Lucifer…I don't want to fight you…" Another step—ssss, click— "I want to help!"

The Devil's stance did not change but his eyes hardened as a smile came and went on his face like a vicious rumor. "I'm not Lucifer any longer, Sitri. Call me Satan."

"I'm serious, Lucifer. Just listen to me, would you? And stop glaring. It makes me nervous." Sitri said and crossed his arms at his chest. "I know what you're trying to do. You know I can help with the cunt." Sitri disliked women. He had no greater pleasure than to coerce them into revealing their secrets and then mocking them for it. Sitri was the bad boyfriend, the mean daddy, the degrading boss.

"Let's catch this train," Sitri said, snapping his fingers. The crowd of people on the platform started, like dreamers coming up from a bad one, and the train could be heard in the tunnel. "We'll talk, all right, Lucifer? Just talk."

The Devil looked from Sitri to the awakening crowd. The riders glanced around, but avoided eye contact with each other. They hefted briefcases higher and pulled jackets closed at their throats. One young woman fumbled her Starbucks and when it hit the platform she burst into tears like an overly tired child. Each would have difficulty shaking the feeling of nightmare that had passed over them this morning.

The Devil nodded at Sitri and Sitri smiled.

"You'll not regret it, Lucifer," he said. But the Devil wondered, nonetheless.

* * *

On the train, no one sat near them. The commuters crowded, herd like, at the opposite end of the car. Sitri smiled at them, a smile wide and dead as a crocodile's and they shuffled uneasily even though none had looked his way.

"Disgusting," Sitri said. He hated humans and only came above to seed dissention and lower self-esteem.

The Devil sat back and tilted his head against the window, closing his eyes. He was calm, but not at ease. He'd have to keep his guard up.

"Why do you despise them so much, Sitri?" he asked. He was hungry again. This body burned fuel as fast as he could fill it.

Sitri shook his head, not taking his eyes from the crowd.

"They have too much. They don't deserve any of it," he said. "They all deserve Hell." The bitterness thickened his voice. The face he'd borrowed drooped into soured lines. The Devil glanced at him with one eye. Sitri looked tired as well as old, not even as spry as he'd been ten minutes before on the platform.

"That's not for us to say," the Devil said.

Sitri cocked his head and looked askance at the Devil.

"Funny thing for you to be saying, Lucifer, considering

where you sit right now."

The Devil only nodded, closing his eyes again.

Sitri cast his attention back to the commuters.

"You know more will go to Heaven than not. Stinking it up. Ruining it. Undeserving shits that they are." His eyes raked the commuters and they swayed, not in time with the rolling train, but blown by Sitri's scorn. "How they can be given Paradise when I…when we…" His hands closed into fists and more than one person felt their heart first constrict and then jump about wildly like a caged rabbit poked with a sharp stick.

The Devil put his hand on Sitri's arm. He felt the familiar depression like a black wave, full of stinging, ruinous salt. He'd not felt so badly since his first five hundred years as Hell's infamous main attendant. He'd sweated and strained under the yoke of the sentence brought down by God, Himself; the very fact of his continued existence a stew of torturous regret and rage.

With force, he turned his mind from it, steering Sitri away as well.

"Did you know Amon and Lillith both tried to bring me back?" he asked. There was no anger in his voice, only curiosity.

Sitri nodded.

"All things serve Him, of course, but those two are both shameless in their currying of favor," he raised his eyebrows. "I think they really do believe there might be a place set for them yet." He shook his head in dismissal of such an idea. "But you are rather a large fish, Lucifer. I am surprised you haven't met with more attempts of repossession."

"I haven't been here very long. Although it seems longer than it's been. They have difficult lives, humans. I'm starting to see that. So much mess and complication. It is as though their brains work at cross-purposes."

"When they work at all," Sitri said, adding a drollness of tone to his voice as he cast a baleful glance at the commuters.

The train screamed into its next stop and birthed the uneasy riders out onto the platform. They scattered, some looking over their shoulders, unable to put a cause to their fear. The young woman with the Starbucks coffee drying in a splatter pattern on her tights flipped open her phone and as soon as she saw daylight, dialed the number of a cab company. She'd decided to take a sick day, but she would be damned if she was riding back to her apartment in that fulminous train.

Sitri wanted to order a car but the Devil merely switched lines to the Patco train that would take them over the bridge and into New Jersey.

"Preposterous," Sitri said, waiting as the Devil bought tickets at a kiosk. "We should not be taking mass transit,

Lucifer. Do you realize how ridiculous you're being? There was a time when we'd have ridden nothing but the blackest of horses, eyes alight with fury…and now you reduce us to this…this…cattle car?"

The Devil made no reply as they settled onto the thin, stingy seats. He glanced at the window but they were underground and he saw nothing save his reflection; it startled him. The thin face–hungry looking and somehow melancholy–was not the picture he had of himself. This face, this body, were vulnerable beyond what he'd ever imagined. Humans were creatures rife with fear and indecision, but how could they not be, carrying themselves in vessels thin-skinned as these?

How could he explain to Sitri that he'd come to understand humans as he'd never been able to do as their punisher. That he'd been both weakened and strengthened in his few short days up here. That he found the longer he was here, the more he wanted to stay.

Once again, Kelly came to mind. The Devil glanced at Sitri, but Sitri was turned away, his mind on something else; he was not causing the Devil to think of Kelly. He wondered if Kelly were thinking of him and that made him feel reduced, and angry. He'd not intended to become so embroiled. So conflicted.

"I need time to build this body. It's weak," the Devil said.

Sitri, noticing the odd tone, turned in his seat to look at the Devil.

"Lucifer," he said, masking his surprise with an amused tone. "I believe you actually like it up here."

The Devil shook his head but turned to look out the window.

"No Sitri, I would not say that I like it. And stop calling me Lucifer. I've not been him for a very long time."

Sitri raised his brows, passing a hand over his magnificent hair.

"Is it really for that lawyer that you've come here? You've risked much," he said. "When I heard, I thought that it could not be. You know there are a few liars amongst our kind." He grinned. "I thought it some sort of fancy one of the lesser minions was spreading. And I pitied whoever had started the slur against you...you of all the ranks! The most steadfast, dedicated–well, I just had to see it for myself. And here you are! It wasn't a tale after all! But, Lucifer, I will ask you again: why?"

"Sitri, stop calling me Lucifer." He closed his eyes against the sudden glare as the train rolled out onto the bridge. "I'm not Lucifer anymore."

* * *

"Carrie! I'm so glad you answered!" Thomas leaned

back in his chair, cell phone to his ear. He couldn't believe Carrie didn't have a cell phone. He'd had to call and call at her trailer until he just happened to catch her at home. Another pain in the ass aspect of the little bitch. "We haven't talked in so long, I've missed you!"

"Thomas, holy shit!" she said and he could hear a dog yapping in the background. Something small. Unease whispered through him at the idea of a vulnerable creature in her care.

"Got yourself a dog, I hear," he said, the smile fading from his face if not his voice. "How's that going?"

"Oh, well…I thought it would be fun, but, it's kind of a pain in the ass, to tell you the truth. Do you know how much these things shit? The people next door were always after me to pick up its crap. 'Oh, Carrie,' they'd say 'your little dog is pooing on our patio again, do you think you could walk her out near the road or maybe keep her on a lead when she's out?' Whining bitches. And it fucking yaps like a motherfucker until I feed its ass." There was a crackling on the line and he realized she'd turned away from the phone. "Shut the fuck up, Paris!" she said and her voice echoed hollowly. There was a sharp yelp and then silence.

"It went in the bedroom. We can talk now," she said. "Sooo, what's going on? I've missed you! Did you see the messages on your blog? Are you on Facebook yet?"

He was taken aback by her cozy enthusiasm. They hadn't talked in more than eighteen months and here she was, acting like he'd just got home from vacation. She really did scare him with her unpredictability.

"I did see your comments on the blog! Very, uh, insightful. Very informative," he said. "It's always great to know someone is on my side out there." His voice, at least, sounded sincere. "But that's actually what I wanted to talk to you about, Carrie."

"Oh really? I kinda thought that might be why you were calling," her voice dipped into a lower register. "Been thinking about me, haven't you?"

"In a way, yes; yes I have," he said. "I was thinking we needed to get together for a little chat."

Her laugh was deep and throaty and practiced.

"Any time, any where, love," she said.

He felt as though he'd been transported into a bad eighties romance. He shook his head and rolled his eyes.

"Well, how about if you come on up here and I'll take you somewhere nice for lunch?"

"Me? Come up there?" she said, and now all the ersatz flirtation deserted and a new voice lashed out: iron hard, demanding, cold. "Dude, you're like a two hour ride from here. For lunch? Fuck you, man. I don't need lunch that bad."

He was stunned by the quick shift in her demeanor. Of

course he'd seen it before. He'd watched her go from an unconcerned, nail-picking, eye-rolling, cold-blooded murderer outside the courtroom to a sweet young girl steamrolled by the horrible circumstances of her life when she was where the jury could see her. But he hadn't had to deal with her in a long time. It brought home to him all over again that he'd set a monster free. Well, the jury had, really. It had been their decision. It wasn't his fault.

"I didn't mean you'd have to drive yourself up," he said. "I'd send a car for you. And I just didn't want to take up too much of your time, that's why I suggested lunch! How about dinner? Would you be available?" God, she was a nightmare. How was he going to ease her out of his life? She came back as regularly as bad weather.

Silence on the other end.

"Carrie?" he said.

Silence.

"Carrie?"

Carrie stood looking at the receiver in her hand. Her face had taken on a shuttered look. Thomas' voice peeped and squawked at her. Was he fucking with her or what? There had been something…false…in his tone. Carrie knew false when she heard it.

"Gosh, that would be great," she said. Her voice had softened into the tones of a very young girl, easily impressed.

Thomas was thrown again by the shift. How did she pass so quickly through each persona? Did she really think no one would notice? He shuddered at the crazy leaking through his telephone line.

"Okay, great!" he said. "How about Wednesday, does that sound good? I'll have the car collect you at three and I'll make reservations somewhere nice. And we'll talk."

"Sounds all kinds of great, lover," she said, Marilyn-breathy. "By the way," she continued, her voice hardening. "That fucking car had better be here right at three or you can kiss my ass."

Now it was his turn to pull the phone from his ear and he stared at it, gape-mouthed. He realized that she actually scared the living shit out of him.

* * *

It was still morning when the Devil and Sitri exited the high-speed line. Nauseous with hunger, the Devil stopped at the first place they found open. It was called Thomasello's Family Pizza and at this time of day they were serving breakfast, mostly to a steady stream of construction workers who took their food to go. The booths and tables were deserted.

The Devil bought six egg sandwiches, handing one to Sitri and paying with Kelly's card.

They retreated to a booth at the back and the Devil tore into the sandwiches. The yolks burst open and dripped onto his hands and the table. Sausage crumbled juicily between his teeth and cheese strung golden and melted from his mouth back to the bun. The Devil nearly hummed with satisfaction.

Sitri watched with mild disgust as the Devil ate. His sandwich sat before him, not yet touched, its wrapping dotted with grease stains.

"Enjoying your food?" Sitri asked, his tone mild.

The Devil sat back, wiping a hand across his mouth and belched. Egg yolk had streaked across his chin, drying in flakes. He took the sandwich that sat before Sitri, tore the paper from it, and devoured it in four large bites.

Then he belched again.

Sitri rolled his eyes and lit one of his slender brown cigarettes.

"Hey, no smoking in here, buddy," the cook called across to them.

Sitri didn't hesitate in the act of taking a drag from the cigarette. He inhaled deeply and then blew a cloud of smoke.

"What's next, Lucifer? Can we at least hire a car?" he said. He took another drag.

"Hey. Buddy. I'm warning you. Put it out." The cook had come to the counter, brushing aside the teenage girl who'd rung them up.

"The address isn't far from here," the Devil said. "I think you'll make it, Sitri."

"The question is whether I want to, Lucifer, not whether I can."

A portion of the counter flipped up and the cook came through, wiping his hands on a grease-stained apron. He was a big man with no fear of other men. Especially an old fart and his skinny kid.

"You're trying my patience, pal," the cook said.

"I think you want to, Sitri; otherwise you would not have come this far. I think you're intrigued...in spite of yourself." The Devil smiled, one side of his mouth coming up.

Sitri shook his head, his irritation obvious. He opened his mouth to reply, but just then, the cook put his hand on Sitri's shoulder.

As soon as his hand was on the old guy's shoulder, the cook felt a deep, unmanning regret. When the old guy turned to look up at him, his lower belly cramped. He thought he might shit himself. The guy's eyes were...were...

The teen at the counter could only see her uncle's back but she knew something was wrong from his wooden posture. She reached for the phone next to the register, tiptoeing her fingers over, being careful to move slowly.

The man facing her way—the thin blond guy who'd eaten like he hadn't eaten in days—caught her nervous glance and he smiled at her. He nodded. Relief flowed through her and she turned back to the magazine she'd been leafing through. She couldn't really remember what she'd been concerned about.

Sitri turned his attention back to the Devil.

"Do you know this one?" he asked and gestured with his head to the frozen cook.

"I'm not sure, let me…" the Devil slid from the booth and stood in front of the cook. The Devil took the man's face in his hands and lifted it. The cook's eyes were bulging and his eyebrows had climbed nearly to his hairline. His mouth worked but no sound came out. The Devil tilted his own head, as though to kiss the man, but only stared into his eyes. Then he stood back, letting the man's head drop.

"No, he's not coming my way," the Devil said and shuffled through the wrappers on the table. Maybe they should get a few more sandwiches for the road. They'd been delicious. "Not yet, anyway."

Sitri reached up and grabbed the cook's ear. He pulled his head down next to his so the cook's ear was right at his mouth.

"Listen to me, human," Sitri said. His voice whispered along the cook's ear canal like a hot wind in the desert, shriveling and crisping everything it blew across. "If you want some trouble I'll give you all you can handle and more. But I don't think you're going to be very...happy...with the results. You think I am an old man, but I am so much more." His tongue snaked out and it slid, long and sinuous around the cook's throat, twenty inches long, thirty inches long and still it lengthened, winding and tightening.

In his frozen state, the cook was aware of everything but could not move. At the touch of the demon's hard tongue, hot urine trickled down the inside of his leg.

Sitri was excited by the acerbic stink of it and the delicious fear flowing from this man. His tongue tightened, tightened, even as his fingers squeezed the cook's ear. He wanted to keep milking his fear, squeezing it out, lapping it up...

The Devil snapped his fingers in Sitri's face.

"Enough." His tone was mild, but Sitri felt the undercurrent of menace. Lucifer was not someone to be fucked with. He withdrew his tongue and let the man go, turning back to grasp the cigarette he'd left burning at the edge of the table.

"Cook?" the Devil said and waved his hand in the cook's face. The cook had been transfixed, staring at Sitri, but now his gaze went to the Devil.

"Huh?" he said, his voice dulled, trying to take a step

back and staggering.

"I'll take six more of these," the Devil said and gestured to the mess of sandwich wrappers on the table.

"Lucifer! Are you serious?" Sitri said, lighting a fresh cigarette off the old. He looked to the cook as if the cook would commiserate. "That's disgusting. How can you shove so much into that poor body? You're going to break it!"

The Devil hadn't even glanced at Sitri, keeping his attention on the cook.

"Cook? Six more."

Something in the Devil's tone woke the cook enough to get him moving. He retreated across the restaurant and back behind the counter. His niece threw him a distracted smile as he went by.

He cooked in a daze, his hands doing the work by rote. His mouth still hung open. His mind felt as though it had been flushed clean with a strong hose. The drying urine made his balls stick to his leg and he kept kicking out, dislodging them. It became a nervous tick that he carried to his grave.

* * *

A carved wood sign stood at the entrance to the Shawnee Woods Trailer Park. A low cinderblock wall and dead azalea bushes surrounded it. The area was rural, the roads through the park rutted dirt tracks. Pine trees and pin oaks fought for air and sun, creating a dense canopy over the trailers.

The trailers themselves were mostly doublewides. Years and years ago, this had been a vacation spot for people coming to fish the lakes and streams, but it had solidified over time into year-round residences. Mainly older, retired folks lived here and their trailers were nicely kept with flowerbeds and concrete pads for their old Buicks and Fords.

But a few of the trailers stuck out due to their run down and over used condition. It was in one of these dilapidated homes that Carrie Walsh lived.

Next to her trailer was a dirt side yard that contained a picnic table so gray and warped with age it seemed carved from driftwood. Dog turds littered the area around the table, along with Styrofoam cups, three empty Boone's Farm bottles, a magazine so bloated with moisture that it was almost the size of an encyclopedia, and a whitewashed car tire.

The Devil and Sitri stood at the entrance to the trailer park, next to the wooden sign.

The Devil's head was up and cocked in a listening posture. He had one arm across Sitri's chest, preventing him from continuing down the dirt drive.

Sitri was irritated. This old body was not holding up to

the walking they'd been doing and he'd run out of the little brown cigarettes it craved.

"What is it, Lucifer? Why are we stopping?" His tone was querulous. He brushed his hair back, patting it into place. "We're nearly there. I'm tired. This body needs a—"

The Devil shook his head, left and then right. If he'd had hackles they would have risen. Now Sitri caught the Devil's tension and his manner changed, his theatrical disdain draining away. He looked down the road and then back to the Devil, quiet and alert.

Late afternoon sun flashed across the Devil's face and his eyes glowed orange.

"Someone is here," he said. An undercurrent of glee threaded his voice. He rolled his shoulders. "Let's go."

They came around the last bend and the trailer sat before them. The sun had gone behind the trees, but a weak light still filled the sky. Six beings stood shoulder to shoulder at the edge of Carrie's dirt-patch, dog turd-littered yard.

Sitri hesitated, nearly stumbling. He'd never seen this many Patrons together. Amabilis and Patroclus guarded against demonic possession and he could guess they were here because of him; he hadn't told the Devil that the circumstances of his habitation of this body were not quite within the rules of the game.

Christina stood next to Dymphna. Hermes and Maturinus were closest to the trailer. Those four were the Patrons of the insane. That there should be four of them just for one woman…it made Sitri's borrowed body's blood run cold.

The Devil stood, hands on his hips and tilted his head back. He closed his eyes and drew in a breath, as though scenting the six Patrons. Then he lowered his head and opened his eyes, smiling. Patrons were not strong creatures as they had once been humans, but this many together—they might pose a problem.

Amabilis was the first to come forward. He floated over the ground, not even stirring the dust beneath his feet. He'd once been human, and though he occupied his original body, it was ghostly and ethereal. He was dressed plainly in robes and cowl befitting his era of death. He was mild looking, especially in comparison to Patroclus behind him, whose stance and manner were that of a warrior at the ready. Patroclus dealt with the more malevolent demons. Along with being taken aback, Sitri was also a bit flattered…both of them? Just for me?

"Amabilis, you are looking gloomier than ever," the Devil said. "Is the work wearing you down?"

Amabilis' eyes welled with tears, making them deep black pools of disillusionment but still he smiled.

"The 'work' as you say, is my calling, my contribution. Difficult though my work may be, it is God, Himself that

I serve and I do so with a joy that sings from my heart."

The Devil rolled his eyes.

"Amabilis, do you never tire of hearing your own rhetoric?"

Amabilis shimmered briefly but smiled again, hands out and palms up.

"Could I tire of serving God, Himself? No. I could not," he said. "Not as you tired of it, of course; going against God, Himself, as you did." He tilted his head and his smile became a caricature of commiseration. "How do you feel that's working out for you now, Satan?"

The Devil's smiled disappeared and his features turned stony.

"You know very little, Patron," the Devil said. His voice had flattened and Sitri felt a swelling fear course through his borrowed body. "You are a mere sycophant trying to worm your way nearer His throne. You want what you cannot have, what you can never have. And it makes you bitter inside. No, Amabilis, you'll never be an Angel, no matter how long or how much you weep for the humans, because you are, yourself, a mortal of the earth."

The smile finally left Amabilis' face, replaced with a small moue of pique. He shrugged his robed shoulders, causing himself to shimmer almost to invisibility.

"Let us not play these games with each other, Satan," Amabilis said. "Suffice to say that I am very troubled, seeing you here."

"I'm not," Patroclus said from behind him.

The Devil glanced at Patroclus and nodded brief acknowledgement.

"And you, Patroclus," he said. "I am surprised to see you here as a mere spear carrier for Amabilis. I thought your place would be at the head of your own helm, not slinking along behind a lesser Patron, tongue at the ready to clean his ass."

Patroclus floated forward, his face pulling into lines of anger, but Amabilis raised a steadying hand.

"Save your taunts, Satan," he said. "Dismayed as I am by the display of your disregard for His demands by deserting your post, Patroclus and I are not here for you."

Amabilis directed his gaze past Satan to Sitri.

"It is Sitri we seek," he said.

Sitri ran his hands over his hair and raised his chin. The Devil glanced at Sitri and then back to Amabilis.

"What is it you want of him?" he said. "This cause and his part in it are no concern of yours."

"Ah, but I'm afraid it is, Satan. Sitri has broken the rules by taking a body not destined for death."

The Devil was surprised but held his feelings close.

"This body?" he said and gestured to Sitri. "Oh, please. If it was not destined at the exact time he took it, surely it was not far off. I think we can call this one a wash."

Amabilis shook his head.

"Of course we cannot 'call this a wash'. There is a soul in that body, Satan, and it is in torment!"

Amabilis' eyes shone again with unshed tears and the Devil was reminded that this was why he detested the Patrons. Their immersion. Their involvement with the dailyness of human need. Their inability to ever get beyond their own mortal beginnings. So what if Sitri had taken a sinner minutes or even hours before his time? So what if its soul was in torment? It deserved all of that and more.

"The torment of the soul of that sinner is nothing as to what it will receive when it is mine in Hell, Amabilis. It is no less than what it deserves."

"That is where you are mistaken, Satan," Amabilis said. "That soul was not earmarked for the nether world. And neither was it set on dying."

The Devil turned and looked at Sitri full on. He raised his eyebrows in a question.

Sitri ran his hands through the magnificent head of hair one more time. He looked from the Devil, to Amabilis and then back to the Devil. He smiled a strained smile.

"I just…I liked this one," he said and the Devil took a breath that expanded his chest, even as his eyes closed. "It's so…it fits me, Lucifer, you can see that! Surely you can even if the Patrons are too—"

The Devil turned, giving Sitri his back and cutting him off.

Looking past Amabilis, thinking hard, the Devil addressed the other four Patrons, his voice stern.

"And you? You would protect the soul of that worthless woman? That murderer of her own baby?"

Christina the Astonishing stirred and floated forth. She and the others had watched the exchange between the Devil and Amabilis with interest but had not participated. Given the choice, they'd not fight Satan at all; but given the circumstances, it seemed they might have to.

"Satan," she said. "You more than any other being in existence understand that it is God, Himself, who commands us. What we do, we do only according to His will."

The Devil shook his head in obvious disgust.

"You are all the same: all Patrons, all mortals. You presume to know the will of God, Himself? Never has He spoken to one of you; no mortal could withstand His voice, not even one designated with a wisp of the divine as you Patrons imagine yourselves to be. What you think you know…you only presume."

Christina smiled. It was a slow and pitying smile, worse than the false commiseration of Amabilis. She would pity him? Unthinkable.

"Christina," the Devil said and now his voice was quiet,

barely audible as the last vestiges of light leeched from the sky. "You are Astonishing only to other mortals. The rest of us–who have known God, Himself and who have sat near to His throne even as you whine at the gate like a stray dog–we find you merely Annoying.

"Now listen and mark me well, Patrons," the Devil continued. "I am going into that trailer and the miserable huddle of human flesh I will find in there is going to lead me to my true quarry. And you will not stop me."

The Devil and Sitri stood facing the six wraithlike Patrons. Neither side moved. Then Sitri sighed in irritation and stepped forward, as if determined to get the upcoming nastiness well behind him.

Amabilis and Patroclus fell upon him, elongating and disappearing up his nose and into his mouth. Sitri's borrowed body flew back, eyes wide and stumbling and landed on its ass. He grunted and bent forward, trying to grab the ground before him as he was dragged backward. He could not get purchase as the Patrons inside the body flipped it up and over, face down in the dirt and kicking.

The other four Patrons came forward and ringed the Devil. They stayed a small distance back, shifting and shimmering, looking for an opportunity into the body the Devil occupied. It would most likely take all four to dislodge Satan. His powers were far beyond that of any regular demon and the Patrons still felt terror at the aspect of losing their immortal souls.

Christina came forth, elongating as she did so, and the Devil tracked her with his eyes. She flew to within two feet of him and he reached for her, but her maneuver was a ruse. Dymphna came around from behind the Devil, even as Christina feinted quickly left.

Dymphna was partly up the Devil's nose, thinning more as she went. Christina rushed back in, aiming for the other nostril, when the Devil met her eyes and winked. She stopped in astonishment and hung suspended, a foot from the Devil's face. She watched in mounting horror and the Devil heaved in a breath that pulled Dymphna all the way in. Then he smiled. He reached out and put his hand into Christina's midsection, holding her in place with his fist even though she had no real substance. He drew her to him as she struggled in his grip. He brought her face close to his.

The Devil's eyesockets had emptied and become windows to the flaming, charnel pits of Hell. Christina could see Dymphna within the Devil's eyes and Dymphna was the picture of torment. She turned and twisted with the damned, buffeted by flames, getting her first, truly close up view of the sinners condemned by God, Himself, to an eternity of burning.

The Devil grinned widely at Christina, his face bathed in an orange and flickering glow.

She cried out and struggled harder in the Devil's grip. At her cries, Hermes and Maturinus came forward but at the Hell burning from Satan's eyes, they were stayed. Hermes was an ancient Saint, having died a martyr in Greece and Maturinus was not much younger. Neither had ever had a chance to witness the Devil, Himself made flesh, much less contemplated trying to best him in battle.

Christina lashed in the Devil's grip and bade them come to her aid and again, they pressed forward.

Behind the Devil, Sitri's borrowed body was whipped to and fro, leaving the ground entirely, seemingly in defiance of gravity itself. His eyes had rolled back into his head as if to witness the spectacle within.

Sitri fought in desperation for the body he'd possessed. Being pushed from it now would cause him an untenured stay back in the charnel pits.

Amabilis and Patroclus expanded themselves and a holy light began to seep from Sitri's pores, pushing him farther from the soul that cowered in the nether regions of this body. He was losing his grip on this plane.

Amabilis bade the soul to fight for itself, to fight the demon possession, but it merely trembled in the darkness Sitri had strung it in.

Patroclus forced himself further and further into the outer reaches of the body and the light glowed brighter, illuminating the Devil ten feet away.

The Devil still held Christina and now he'd also gripped the insubstantial form of Hermes, but that was a mistake. Christina and Hermes pushed against each other and the Devil struggled to hold them together. They pushed his arms wide and as he cried out in frustration, Maturinus slid into his mouth.

The Patron knitted himself to the Devil's arm and weakened it. Maturinus pulled free and flew in a frenzy between the Devil's gritted teeth. He enmeshed himself in the muscles of the Devil's neck and brought his head back, pulling him over. The Devil landed hard on his back and lost his grip on Christina.

She flew into his gasping mouth.

His diaphragm had tightened when he fell and now she was constricted within it. Then the Devil pulled in a breath and she continued down to his legs.

Behind the Devil, Sitri's body was wracked with tremors so violent that they had cracked six of the body's false teeth. The glorious pompadour was dusty and tangled. But the former occupant's soul was finally shaking itself awake as if from a nightmare.

The Patrons' holy God light had finally reached it.

The Devil heaved himself up, fighting against the numbness coursing into him as the Patrons fought for control of Mark's body. He staggered to his knees, howling, and pushed himself upright. Leaning over, hands on his thighs, he began to heave. Hot light shot from his eyes and his mouth opened wide, pulling his jaws apart nearly to the breaking point.

He heaved again, his diaphragm becoming rigid as iron, his stomach nearly touching his backbone.

He heaved again.

Behind him, the body Sitri occupied had grown still, but something began to whistle from deep within it. It began as a teakettle whistle, hesitant and stuttering, right before the water is ready to boil. Then Sitri's head dropped slowly to the left and his mouth hung open and the whistle became louder, stronger; now a teakettle at medium boil. The white light still shone from the body and now it had puddled around it like ground fog, ghostly blue-white.

Amabilis and Patroclus appeared in the light around Sitri's body, wearily condensing from the leaden glow.

Now the teakettle was a whistle at full boil and then it shot through the registers, climbing higher, getting louder. Now it sounded like a train half a mile from the depot and getting closer. Amabilis and Patroclus floated tiredly to one side, watching sternly and resignedly, seemingly unbothered by the fever pitch train whistle.

The whistle got as loud as it seemed it could get, drowning out the world, and all at once, Sitri appeared next to the body. The whistle died away into a line of faint, breathless squeaks as the body's chest deflated.

Sitri glanced at the ghostly Patrons and threw a petulant kick at the old man's body lying prone in the dirt. The kick did not connect: Sitri had become an apparition, too. Though he looked eerily like the Patrons, he was not one of them. The Patrons, who occupied only themselves, could stay as they pleased and without a body, Sitri would soon disappear.

Sitri would Transition.

He turned his back and sat cross-legged in the dirt and pine needles. A stray cat wandered close to sniff his transparent hand and Sitri moodily waved it away. Already he was feeling isolated and lost. It was a crushing, demeaning feeling of utter despair and hopelessness that a Patron would never have to feel. And therefore, would never understand.

Patroclus faded first, never sparing a glance to the Devil's struggle behind him. He'd done his job here and was anxious to move on. He didn't like being so close to Satan. Amabilis watched the body that Sitri had occupied. The chest rose once and fell. Rose again and fell. Rose again. Now Amabilis began to fade, too, his eyes on the body as he did so. Wishing the old man well. Wishing him Godspeed.

Sitri glanced over his own melting shoulder at the

Devil. He was already beginning to lose interest in how it would come out for Lucifer. One way or another, they'd meet again in Hell. He had no doubt of that.

The Devil was only peripherally aware of the activity behind him as he heaved out the Patrons. They were tenacious, but he was strong, the food and exercise he'd given this body paying off.

Plus, there was no soul in here to help the Patrons in their fight for control—Mark had more than willingly given up this body. There was only him, and he was the Devil: Lucifer and Satan. Loved and scorned. Good and evil. Occupier of all worlds. Uniquely qualified, so he thinks, to make this one, small, judgment.

And they'd not keep him from it.

He heaved again. Blood vessels in his neck stood out and his muscles trembled with effort. With each convulsion, orange light raked the dead leaves and pine needles and they glowed as if on fire. His face grew redder than the inferno within his eyes as capillaries burst under the strain.

Three of the four Patrons shot from his mouth and landed in crumpled disarray at his feet.

The Devil pulled in a breath that nearly stunned his body into a faint and the world swam dizzily around him. He stepped away from the tangle of wraiths and breathed in again, the breath tearing into his lungs, filling them nearly to bursting. The world tilted, but not as badly, and he felt this body coming to rights. Exhaustion bent him double and he put his hands back on his thighs, wearily supporting himself.

Christina was the first Patron to disentangle herself. She was shaken, almost without substance, weakened almost to nonexistence. The Devil saw her only as a light glimmer around her eyes, her mouth, her hands. When she spoke, it was as if she stood miles distant.

"You cannot keep Dymphna in Hell…no saint can be kept there!"

Muffled as her voice was, indistinct as she'd grown, the Devil could still hear the righteous indignation in her voice…and the fear.

His lowered head rose enough that she could see the burning pits of his eyes and she shimmered almost to invisibility.

"Christina," he said, his voice like heavy, rusted chains dragged across gravel. "You forget your place. You have all forgotten your place."

Beneath Christina, Hermes and Maturinus disappeared entirely, slinking away like chicken stealing foxes. Christina looked down and saw that they had fled and she looked back at Satan, eyes flashing brightly. Tears that seemed to phosphoresce slid down her cheeks and dropped, disappearing into the warm night air.

The Devil stood and placed his hands at his lower back. He bent and stretched, sighing and unconcerned, ignoring the saint before him.

"You cannot keep her, Satan!" Her voice had grown teary and ragged. "You cannot keep a Patron in Hell. You must release her at once! I command it! God, Himself, commands it!" A flip of her robe shimmered and settled as though she'd stamped her foot.

He regarded her with stern, dispassionate eyes. "You are not God, Himself, Christina. You do not know what He commands. You can only guess and hope that He has remained on your side. He does not always reward the ones who serve Him, does He, Christina?" He spread his arms wide. "You have overstepped."

He reached for her.

"Satan! Please!" Christina said and now her midsection shimmered as she dropped to her knees. "I beg of you, Satan, please. Please torture Dymphna no more. Everything we do, we do to serve God. Please Satan. In His name, I beg this, in His name…"

The Devil took another deep breath and tilted his head at the groveling Patron. He nodded.

"His will be done, then," he said, sarcasm darkening his words. He placed one finger against his right nostril, pinching it closed and then reared back, drawing in a breath through his mouth. He hesitated, catching

Christina's eye and he winked again.

He bent forcefully forward and expelled the last Patron from his other nostril.

* * *

Christina hovered over the curled form of Dymphna and waved her hands gently in the air above her. Light shimmered where her hands made contact with Dymphna, but it was not a bright light. It was not a healthy light. Christina spoke without looking up.

"We were bid come here, no matter that you believe it or not, Satan," she said. Her voice was deep with grief. "We do not choose the ones we protect, he or she chooses us."

"Your protection of this one is misguided," he said, watching the ritual Christina performed over the dazed Dymphna. Small sparks of pure white light had begun to pop and tumble from Christina's hands, landing on Dymphna and sizzling across her form, as if Christina were trying to ignite her back to consciousness.

"Tell me something, Christina," the Devil said, incredulous curiosity in his voice. "Are you saying that one in there,"–he gestured toward the trailer–"prayed to you?"

"No, not that one. It was another…we were called through an Intervention."

The Devil paused, surprised. An Intervention was a more serious matter. Depending on who had called out for it, God, Himself might even Sanction it. Patron Saints were not bound to very many things, but when God Sanctioned an Intervention, they came in accordance with His wishes.

"Who intervened on her behalf?"

Christina did not answer. She continued her ministrations to Dymphna.

"Christina," the Devil said. "Who would be that imbecilic? That misguided?"

She looked up and now her eyes sparkled with eerily dancing points of light that seemed at once near and impossibly distant; like the milky way at the equator.

"Her son."

* * *

The Devil sat on the old picnic table outside Carrie's trailer. The night had become very dark. There was no moon. He was angry and deeply troubled, torn by his conflicting emotions.

The Patrons had disappeared moments before, leaving him to ponder Christina's last words. They had been astonishing, indeed. The woman's son? The murdered baby? How could that possibly be the case?

But the Devil knew with certainty that the Patron would never have lied; would never have even considered it a possibility for herself to do so.

How could that beaten and abused little boy want to Intervene for his mother? And if he, the wronged, were capable of forgiveness then shouldn't–

A hand descended on the Devil's shoulder and he jumped, turning. The old man–whom Sitri had so recently been evicted from–stood before him, dazed and swaying. His mouth worked and there were large gaps where his dentures had cracked and crumbled apart.

The Devil considered him.

"What?" the Devil said, his impatience clipping the word short.

"I…I'm…I think I…" the old man said, fumbling over his words. His eyes had a struck look. Stunned.

"Old man, you're making no sense," the Devil said. "Speak or leave me. On second thought, never mind the speaking, just leave."

The Devil turned away.

The old man stood in confusion.

"Young man," he said, placing cold, trembling fingers to the Devil's shoulder. "I believe I may need some help, here. I can't seem to remember…" he looked around, blank-eyed. "…can't seem to remember where I am."

The Devil had lowered his chin into his hand, exasperated at this intrusion.

"You're at the Shawnee Woods Trailer Park," he said. "Lucky you."

Light, sharp fingers tap-tapped on his back.

"Young man? Can you help–"

The Devil rounded on him. He pointed down the dirt road.

"Go that way until you see lights. Knock. Tell them your sad story," he turned away and sat back down. "Go now. I've got bigger fish to fry."

The old man was silent but the Devil could still feel his presence at his back. Then came a low sniffle and a small, mewling sob. He was crying. The Devil put his head in his hands and sighed. For some reason, Kelly came to his mind. Her kindness and pity.

He stood, turned and held out his hand.

The old man wiped his eyes and reached out shakily, and the Devil closed his hand around his. The old man's fingers were thin and they felt as brittle and dry as pretzel sticks.

"Come on then," the Devil said and sighed again. "I'll help you."

The Devil walked him to the next trailer in the line of homes. This one was nicely kept; warm light shone from the windows illuminating lovingly tended flowerbeds. There was an awning that ran almost the entire length and housed a picnic set and stainless steel grill.

The Devil prodded the old man, trying to get him to walk on his own to the trailer, but the old man balked and would not let go of the Devil's hand. Sighing again but also thinking of Kelly, he walked the man to the trailer's door and rapped lightly.

Behind them, a car pulled into the drive, a blue Impala.

"Can I help you boys?" A woman said, turning off the lights and exiting the car.

"Yes, this man…" the Devil said and jumped down from the steps. He pushed the old man lightly forward. "He could use some help. A phone, perhaps? He seems to have mislaid himself."

The lady studied the old man's face and then her eyes slid to the Devil's. She bent back into her car and grabbed a grocery bag then stepped up to her door and unlocked it. She pushed it open invitingly.

"Well, sure thing. Bring him on in here. Poor old soul."

The Devil set his jaw but led the old man past the lady and into the trailer. What was another few minutes of distraction after all the distraction he'd faced thus far? It was as nothing, he thought, and smiled grimly to himself.

"Here honey, set right down in the kitchenette. Let me get you a glass of something." She was moving around the tiny kitchen having deposited the bag on the counter. "Water? Or do you think a little nip of something more medicinal?" She rooted in a lower cabinet and stood to wiggle a brown bottle temptingly. She smiled. "I'm Edy, by the way, Edy Sommers. And you are…?" She was looking at the old man, but he shook his head and dropped it into his hands, his elbows propped on the table.

She turned to the Devil, who had remained standing and was now trying to inch back out the door.

"What's your dad's name, honey?" she said. "Does he like whiskey? I also have Sambucca…think he might like that better?"

"He's not my father, actually," the Devil said. "I was just visiting a friend and he was wandering–"

"Oh ho! That's just terrible!" she said and poured the whiskey into a small glass and set it in front of the old man. When he didn't respond, she pushed it a few inches closer and then turned expectantly to the Devil, her eyebrows raised. "Who's your friend, honey?"

"She lives next door to you; Carrie Walsh," he said and reached behind him for the doorknob. "I think I should probably get back over there–"

Edy's face drew up in disgust and she turned away. She tapped the whiskey glass millimeters closer to the old man. She shrugged.

"Not much cause for you to go rushing off," she said. "Carrie isn't home. She left earlier today."

A crashing anger ripped into the Devil and his eyes glowed briefly with infernal light. He turned away and faced the door. He considered ripping it from the frame and throwing it out into the night.

Controlling his voice, he said:

"Really? And did she tell you where she was going?"

"She was miss high and mighty, I can tell you that much! Big 'ol black limo here for her. She made a big show of it too; delaying to make sure everyone got a good look at her with the car. Pranced around with that poor little dog of hers, telling it to go poo because she didn't have all day. She had somewhere to be! All la-di-da and waving like Miss America at anyone who had the misfortune to go past."

She glanced at the Devil.

"I'm sorry to say those things, her being your friend and all, but I have to speak my mind. I always have."

The Devil nodded.

"I understand. But she didn't say where she was going?"

"Oh, some lawyer friend of hers had sent the car, so she told me. He was fetching her up to la-di-da Princeton to take her out for dinner and dancing. Big romantic hoo-raw."

Gratitude flowed through him, making his knees weak and he thought of Kelly again. Had he not been thinking of her—of her kindness—and helped the old man…he would never have found the answer he sought.

He put a hand on Edy's shoulder and she turned and smiled up at him, laying her hand over his.

"I really am sorry, honey; I mean that. The other neighbors and I have some crazy ideas about the things she's done but…well, she's your friend and I shouldn't have said anything so off-color. Will you accept my apology?"

He smiled.

"Only if you'll do me a favor," he said.

"Anything, honey; what is it?"

"I have to leave…will you help this man? Help him find his way home?"

"Oh shoot, I can do that and it isn't a favor to you! It's just what any decent human would do, don't you think so?"

* * *

A dusty red Sentra pulled onto the shoulder just past where the Devil stood. It was very early, the sky just beginning its transition from deep blue to pearly pinkish gray.

The driver leaned out his window and called back:

"You need a lift, son?"

The Devil got into the passenger side and closed the door, but the driver continued to look at him expectantly. The Devil raised his eyebrows at the driver.

"Son," the driver said. "Don't you want to bring your cat along with you?"

The Devil controlled his features and looked to his right. A mottled gray tomcat sat on the shoulder staring up at him. As he watched, the cat stood on its hind legs and batted at the door handle, all the while never losing eye contact with the Devil.

Sitri? The Devil thought and the cat sat down, still staring at him steadily.

The Devil opened the door and the cat jumped nimbly onto his lap. Its fur was tattered and dirty; it was obviously an animal that had spent its life outdoors. One ear was torn raggedly down the side, giving it a ruffled appearance. It stared at the Devil, unblinking yellow eyes glowing mildly in the dawn light.

It is you, Sitri, isn't it? the Devil thought. The cat blinked slowly and then bounded from his lap to the back seat. The Devil turned to look at him and the cat blinked again. Then it winked.

Putting oneself in an animal was almost unheard of, especially for higher-ranking demons, and the Devil was surprised that Sitri had done it. Animals were uncomfortable and confining and their base instincts tended to stick with the possessor. It would not be an ideal situation to be made to lick one's own balls, want to chase mice, or to be dependent on humans. To make himself so vulnerable, Sitri must have been desperate to stay on earth…but why?

They stopped shortly thereafter at a fast food restaurant, but got their food to go. Now the well at the Devil's feet was strewn with garbage. He'd eaten prodigiously—as had Sitri—as the driver had looked on with easygoing alarm.

Sitri you should be pleased, the Devil thought as he stared out the window at the passing scenery. It's not a black horse, but it is transport, at least. He smiled ruefully and glanced at the cat curled on the deck under the back window.

Me, my cat Sitri, and Bill Bixby, he thought, shaking his head, heading north.

"Bet you thought I was making it up about my name, didn't you?" The man half-grinned at the Devil but didn't take his eyes from the road. He looked to be in his mid-fifties. He was in a suit and tie, but the suit looked rumpled and a bit ill-used. "Everyone thinks I'm making it up," he said and shook his head with self-satisfaction. "But I'm not!"

The Devil said nothing, merely continued staring as the scenery changed gradually from pine forests and farms to strip malls and gas stations. The gas stations and stores popped up slowly at first with long distances separating them but the further north they went, they appeared with accumulating frequency.

"My father was Bill Bixby, his father was Bill Bixby…shoot, we've been Bill Bixbys since before Bill Bixby was born! It's fun, though. People ask me: 'you gonna Hulk out, Bill?' and sometimes I growl at them, you know, just as a little joke."

There was a weight on the Devil's eyelids, pulling them down. He crossed his arms at his chest and tilted his head back onto the headrest.

"Tired?" Bill asked him; somewhat stupidly, the Devil thought.

"Yes," the Devil said.

"Probably all those sandwiches you ate. You're going into a food coma. Your cat is already in one!" Bill Bixby laughed and it was startling: a hearty 'haw! haw!' followed by a wheeze. "Get your rest, we've got about another hour or so. Probably you're wondering why I took these local highways instead of the turnpike, well I'll tell ya, I think…"

The Devil felt his consciousness waning. Bill's voice floated in and out.

"…driving too fast and…"

He slipped further down, on the very edge of sleep.

"…those semis taking up too much road…"

The Devil slept.

He dreamed first of the Patrons. Their sorrowing eyes

loomed large before him and stared at him meaningfully as though they wanted him to see something he'd missed. In his dream, he waved them away, angry and annoyed and his body jerked reflexively.

Then he slipped into another dream where he sat beside a hospital bed. His attention was focused on a pill cup sitting on the bedside table. He had a deep desire for whatever was in there. The feeling was almost that of being thirsty, but so much stronger—it was the apex of thirst.

"Mark," a voice said and it was muffled and weak. He recognized the voice but it was unimportant. The important thing was in that pill cup. It nearly sang with possibility, with promise. His arm floated up as though he had no control over it; as though it was not he who reached for the pill cup.

"Mark, I'm glad you came."

The voice again. Now the Devil fought to turn his head. To see who lay in the bed, even though he knew already who would be there…it was Kelly, in a hospital bed, and she was badly hurt. Why couldn't he turn his head? And he realized it was because Mark hadn't turned to look at Kelly. He'd only wanted the pill. This wasn't a dream; this was Mark's memory.

His hand reached out to the pill cup.

"Mark, what are you doing? You can't take that. That's

for me…Mark, please."

Her voice was dissolving into tears. He wanted desperately to stay his (Mark's) hand and turn his head. He needed to see Kelly, needed to help her, find out what had happened…

He jerked himself awake, sitting up, arm reaching out.

"Whoa there, son," Bill said. "Take it easy, okay? Anyway, like I was saying about the turnpike…they have this part where it splits–trucks go one way and cars the other–but cars can go on the truck side, and let me tell you, when I see a car picking the truck side I think to myself 'now there goes a guy or gal with a death wish,' because those trucks just…"

He tuned the driver out, realizing he'd barely been asleep. The dream was disturbing and at first, he wondered if it meant Kelly was hurt. But no, it was something he'd accessed in Mark's subconscious, from his memories. Although, she had been hurt at some point, badly enough to be in the hospital. What had happened and when had it happened? A fierce protectiveness washed through him that until now he would have attributed to having possessed her brother's body. Now he wasn't sure. The protectiveness seemed purely his own, especially in light of Mark's callous disregard for her.

He tightened his arms over his chest and closed his eyes again, chasing sleep.

* * *

Thomas Evigan stared in disbelief at the girl standing in his lobby. Carrie was wearing skintight jeans with black lace inlay that ran up the sides, exposing her skin to the waist on both sides of her body. She wore high heel boots that came to her knees and flared out ridiculously at the top, like pirate boots. A denim vest covered with a white, crocheted shrug that barely covered her bare shoulders completed her outfit. Her arm jangled with mis-matched bangle bracelets.

She looked like a hooker from 1985.

His mouth had dropped open and she tilted her head back and laughed.

"I look that good, huh?" she said, her voice throaty and confidential. "Yeah, I thought you would like this outfit. Plus, since we're going somewhere fancy, I figured I better class it up."

He recovered himself and came forward, his hand out.

"Carrie, so good to see you! You look great!" He reached to shake her hand but she bypassed it and stepped into him, her arms going around his neck. She reached to kiss his mouth and he turned his face at the last second and kissed her cheek as she kissed his. He stepped back and her arms fell. She stood awkwardly, staring at him with drawn-together brows.

He cleared his throat.

"You look gorgeous! You've certainly been taking care of yourself. That outfit is very…it's so…" In his mind, he was scrapping the reservations he'd made at a very prominent restaurant and decided to take her to a local brewery instead. He'd have to get Kelly to make the change, but he couldn't let this little mongoose hear— she'd know she was being slighted. She had an ear for it.

"It's so what?" she said and her hands went to her hips. Her eyes narrowed. "It's so what, Thomas? Do you like it or not? If you don't, then you're just a douche that don't understand fashion." She glanced at Kelly, but Kelly was bent over a file, minding her own business.

Thomas, who purchased hand-tailored suits and even had his French cuff shirts custom made, inwardly rolled his eyes. This was going to be a long night.

"I was going to say that it's so fresh; so youthful. You really wear it well. Everyone at the restaurant is going to be green with jealousy that you're with me." He reached for her hand and smiled. "Come back to my office. It's early yet and I wanted to talk with you a bit…get caught up."

He settled her in his office and came back to where Kelly sat in reception.

He leaned over her and whispered his instructions,

telling her to cancel Chateau Fleming and instead book a back table at the Alden Brother's Brewery. Carrie watched from behind the half open door of his office, taking in their intimate postures. So it was like that, huh? He liked that revolting receptionist? Her eyes narrowed again. She wasn't going to let that ugly ass bitch interfere with her plans. Not on her life.

Thomas straightened so she stepped back from the door and slid into the chair behind his desk. She sat back, bringing her legs up and crossing them at the ankles, her boots scattering pens and crumpling papers. She grabbed each boob and lifted them higher in her push-up bra and pressed them together in the v of her vest. Then she tossed her hair forward so it looked thicker (she'd seen that in a movie) and she waited for him to enter.

But instead of Thomas, the ugly bitch receptionist stuck her head through the door.

"Miss Walsh, Thomas asked me to tell you that he'd be just a minute. Can I get you a water or coffee?" Kelly smiled and it was such an open, friendly smile that it soured Carrie's stomach.

Carrie brought her feet down with a bang and tilted forward, hands on the desk. "Yeah, get me water, and not tap water either; bring me some of the fancy shit they must keep around here–that sparkling shit. And it better be cold. Or I'll tell Thomas to fire your ass." Carrie had to let this chick know that she, Carrie, held all the cards. No one put on the high and mighty act when Carrie was around. She was queen fucking bee and they better not forget it.

Kelly left and returned with a small bottle of Perrier and a glass filled with ice and set them down in front of Carrie. She smiled. Carrie read pity in her smile, almost a sad commiseration, and it infuriated her. Who was this bitch to pity her? Who was she kidding?

Kelly left without a word.

Carrie swigged directly from the bottle and gagged. This water tasted terrible! Hard and minerally. Thomas walked in as she choked and sputtered.

"Are you all right?" he asked, but did not come around to her. Even in her distress, she noted this.

"I think your secretary tried to poison me! This water tastes like chemicals!" Carrie jumped up, wobbling slightly on her pirate heels. "What the fuck? What kind of losers do you have fucking employed here?" She backhanded the glass of ice, sending it sprawling, shooting ice across the desk top.

Thomas watched the ice fly and saw the crumpled papers, expensive pens on the floor, and he felt hot rage course through him. He strode forward and grabbed the bottle from her hand.

"Kelly!" he called over his shoulder and swigged quickly

from the bottle. "There's nothing wrong with this," he said to Carrie, hissing viciously, "it's just mineral water, you dumb hick."

Kelly walked in.

"Yes, Thomas?"

"Kelly," he said, keeping his eyes on Carrie as she'd sunk back down into the chair, a slapped expression contorting her features. "Could you bring us some paper towels? Ms. Walsh has had a little accident."

He felt he'd scored a victory, putting the little hellion in her place. Certainly she was quieter, more subdued. He was glad he'd taken her in hand and glad that he'd done it by insulting her. Her type; it's what they understood. Rule by the fist.

* * *

They were at a back booth in the brewery and from where they sat they could see the bar and the enormous, stainless steel tanks of beer behind it. The shiny pipes running in a dizzying maze around the tanks made the entire operation look like a bright Geiger. The three bartenders handed out small paper cups of the microbrews for customers to taste as they ate their fish and chips or country-style potpies.

This was a busy place, but Carrie and Thomas were out

of the way and it was quieter, more private.

Thomas was looking over the menu, feeling very self-satisfied. He'd found the key, he thought, to talking to Carrie. He'd merely had to show her who was the boss and now she'd acquiesced to him. He couldn't understand why he'd been afraid of her before. She really was just a dumb hick.

The waitress came to the table and when Carrie opened her mouth to order, Thomas spoke over her.

"We'll each have the house salad, with the house dressing on the side, and meatloaf with the steamed vegetables instead of the mashed potatoes." He pulled Carrie's menu from her unresisting hands, put it with his and handed them both to the waitress. "A Saratoga for me and tap water for the lady." He smiled insultingly at Carrie.

Carrie closed her mouth with a snap and bowed her head.

Thomas felt another thrill of victory. This would make telling her to back off just that much easier. She was completely cowed. He was delighted. He failed to notice—or chose not to—the cold, speculative glance she gave him. Her eyes were as dead as a shark's, flat and ominous.

He decided to start right in and get it over with so he could then enjoy his meal. The waitress poured the bottle of Saratoga into his glass and the bubbles clung nervously to the side. She poured tap from a metal pitcher into Carrie's glass. Thomas raised his glass in a salute and when Carrie didn't raise her drink, he wiggled his at her.

"Sip?" he said and then laughed. "Okay, seriously. Let me tell you why you're here, Carrie."

He sat back and took a breath, looking up. This was his 'getting ready to tell someone the cold hard facts for their own good' stance. Carrie recognized it from the times they'd consulted at the jail. Her lips twitched in the barest hint of a sneer. Thomas was too busy getting air for his pontification to notice.

"It's like this, Carrie," he began on an outward rush of breath. It made him sound as though he deeply regretted having to say what he was about to say but it was for the best of his listener. "You have to move on with your life. There is no 'you and I', no 'we', and you're just going to have to accept it. I don't want you posting anything on my blog, I don't want you calling me, I don't want you emailing me or trying to contact me through the website. Listen, I know you're grateful. I helped you out of a jam and now you think I'm your knight in shining armor…it's not uncommon, believe me!" He chuckled, shaking his head. "I know the effect I have on my clients!"

Carrie had yet to speak or touch the salad the waitress had set before her while Thomas lectured. She had glanced at the waitress, noting the woman's embarrassed expression. Embarrassed for her. That was infuriating. Her hands twisted and gripped on each other under the table.

"You and I are really from different worlds." He leaned in, his lapels nearly in his salad. "Everyone knows you killed your kid. I'm a lawyer; I can't have scandal like that associated with me. I'm going to be a politician, a big one, and it's going to happen sooner rather than later. You think they wouldn't use something like a relationship with you against me? Especially considering the fact that you're a nutso—"

The waitress cleared her throat, her face was bright red.

"Can I take your salads? Are you through with them?"

"Yes, take them," Thomas said, sitting back.

"Miss?" the waitress asked, "Was there something wrong with your salad?"

Carrie tilted her head back and looked up at the waitress. She was very pretty in a girl-next-door kind of way, with soft, sympathetic brown eyes. She smiled at Carrie encouragingly.

Without taking her eyes from the waitress, Carrie pushed her salad plate onto the floor at her feet. It exploded like a salad bomb. Thomas had been checking his phone and was only aware of the aftermath of the plate on the floor, greens scattered about and oily dressing splashed onto the waitress' shoes. She jumped back, open-mouth with shock. Thomas became annoyed, he assumed she'd dropped the salad as she took it from Carrie's place.

"Well, don't stand there staring at it," he said, "Pick it up! Christ, wake up dummy." He shook his head in disgust. "And get someone over here to clean that floor–that dressing is deadly. I should know; I'm a lawyer. I've sued people over much less." He laughed, not caring that he'd just insulted the waitress and at the same time, unable to understand why she didn't laugh at his joke. His jokes were very funny. Well, but, service people didn't matter much in the scheme of things. Who could be more replaceable?

The waitress looked up at Carrie, gape-mouthed and Carrie smiled at her–a toothy, shark grin ruled by her dead black shark's eyes. A ripple of anger was chased away by a wave of fear and the waitress bent to collect the bits of ceramic. She was suddenly very glad this was the last table of her shift.

Thomas shook his head, irritated by the interruption when his speech had been going so well. Clumsy waitress. A busboy came to her aid and together they got the mess cleaned up and she disappeared back into the kitchen. Another server brought their meatloaf and silently placed it before them.

Thomas stared at the retreating back of the server, shaking his head, thoroughly preoccupied by the poor service he was receiving here tonight.

"It's your secretary, isn't it?" Carrie said. It was the first thing she'd said since the mineral water debacle at his office. Her voice was quiet and even. "That's why you're doing this…it's Kelly, right?"

He glanced at her, distracted. "Huh? Oh, uh, yes, it's Kelly." He thought Carrie was just confirming Kelly's name. He hadn't heard the beginning of what she'd said. "They're really having an off night here. Usually the service is very good. I don't understand it," he said and dug into his dinner. "Anyway, as I was saying…where was I?"

"Politician," Carrie said, her voice was neat and even. She looked at him steadily.

"Uh…oh, yes," he said. "That's right." He looked at her and unease flitted over his features. "So anyway, I'm going to be a politician, a big one. Someday maybe the biggest, if you get my drift." He cocked his head at her and grinned. "You may not know this, but the things I do now will have bearing on my future. I can't have any skeletons and you, well…" He forked in a chunk of meatloaf and shook his head again, chuckling. "You've got a skeleton in your—"

He took a breath and the half chewed chunk of meatloaf lodged in his throat. He tried to get his breath and couldn't. His eyes popped out in panicked surprise and Carrie felt a worm of interest, watching him struggle. Maybe he would die right here. It happened all the time, people choking to death in restaurants. She gave him another speculative look. Might be kind of cool. She'd be able to intimate that they were in a relationship...he wouldn't be able to rebut her from the grave. Maybe she could even get something because of it...part of his estate or something. That would be pretty awesome.

He curled his hand into a fist and punched himself in the diaphragm. It wasn't a very hard hit—you can't punch yourself in the midsection very hard—but it was enough to dislodge the meatloaf. It popped from his mouth and landed in the middle of the table, shining wetly in the candlelight.

He heaved in a ragged breath.

She leaned forward, her features drawing together in concern. He took another breath, preparing to tell her that he was okay. He'd be okay.

"That was so Presidential!" she said, the sarcasm like acid, eating away at the words. "That how they do it in the White House?"

* * *

He stood outside the pub with her and tried to talk her

into his car, but she refused. The night had gotten chilly and the streets were wet with a spring rain that had passed through while they ate.

"I'll call you a cab, how about that? You can stay somewhere in town tonight and then you can take the train back tomorrow."

"Really. Which train is it that goes to my trailer park?" she asked him, but her tone was mild. She wasn't concerned about transportation because she wasn't going home tonight and probably not tomorrow, either. She had a couple pieces of business to attend to. Her little dog Paris flashed across her mind. She hadn't left it any food. Had she left it water? She couldn't remember. Ah shit, well…she could always get another dog. No big deal.

"How about this," he said. "I'll put you up somewhere; a nice place right here in town."

Her mind ticked.

"How much is a nice place?" she asked.

"I'm not sure off-hand. Probably two to three hundred."

"A week?" she asked. The number was astronomical.

He chuckled.

"A night, Carrie. That price would be for one night."

She was really getting tired of his condescension. That shit would not fly once they were married. He'd learn to respect her. She held out her hand.

"Just give it and I'll take care of myself." She thought. "Give me six—enough for two nights."

Now it was his turn to think. Six hundred dollars was a lot of money, but was it a lot to be done with her? No. Not at all. He fished the bills from his wallet.

"Are you sure you'll be all right? I could drive you to—"

"Jesus, Thomas, I'm fine. I can take care of myself, in case you hadn't noticed yet. Just go." Now she was anxious to get rid of him. She wasn't sure what time it was, but she knew she had to get where she was going as quickly as possible. If she was to have a chance.

He gave her a sickly grin and backed away. He keyed his car to life and drove off, waving. She raised her hand briefly. She waited until he turned at the next intersection and then trotted lightly to the alley beside the restaurant. She went to the end and saw a handful of cars lined up across the back of the building. Employee's cars, she figured. She hunkered down in the blackness next to one of the large garbage cans. She pulled a knife from her boot—it was a knife from the restaurant, an eight-inch steak knife. She'd slipped it in there when no one was looking. It was lucky Thomas had gotten them a secluded table.

She waited, her eyes on a screen door she thought would lead to the restaurant's kitchen. She would take care of that nervy bitch of a waitress.

The waitress came through the door and paused half in and half out, propping the door open with her hip. She stood directly under the bare bulb that hung over the small back porch. She reached down and swiped at her feet with a cloth. It looked as though she'd done that more than a few times already.

She shook her head and stood and Carrie could hear the low rumble of a male voice from deeper in the kitchen. Now the waitress laughed.

"Oh, hey, I don't need an excuse to buy shoes, believe me! I just didn't want to have to spend my tips on another pair of work shoes so soon."

She looked at her ruined shoes and the male voice rumbled again.

The waitress looked up and smiled back into the kitchen. Her smile was weary but also sweet and full of kindness. It turned Carrie's stomach.

"No, I'll be fine. I'm just going to go home and put my feet up. Tonight was…a long one."

She waved and turned, letting the screen door shut behind her. She crossed to the row of cars near the alley.

Carrie made a small, mewling sound at the back of her throat. It sounded like a hurt puppy. She'd learned the noise from her own dog. That dog cried a LOT.

She mewled again.

The waitress heard the sound coming from near the dumpsters and her first thought was feral cats—they dug in the garbage all the time—but the feral cats made very little noise. Unless they were fighting or doing it, she thought, then they make plenty of noise!

This sounded more like a kitten, maybe even a puppy in distress. She stood next to her Civic, letting her eyes adjust. She checked her watch...Todd would be wondering where she was if she didn't get going. The mewling came again, a bit louder, as if the animal had sensed her wavering. She sighed. I'll just make sure it's okay. I'm not bringing anything home with me! She walked to the dumpsters, crooning in a soothing way, reassuring any animal that she was no threat.

The waitress said:

"It's okay, I'm not going to hurt you; it's okay baby..."

From her hiding place, Carrie nearly laughed. She brought the back of her knife hand to her mouth to stifle a giggle. The knife stuck straight up from her palm. Dumb bitch, she thought. Just come a little closer, just a little bit...

The waitress inched forward trying to see into the gloom. She was thinking that the poor kitten or puppy was so scared it wasn't even crying anymore.

"Kitty kitty?" she said. "Puppy puppy? Are you still back—"

She saw a glint and her first thought was that it was the animal's eyes, but it would have had to be three feet tall. Then the glint came again and now it was at four feet, now at five, still going higher.

The waitress took one alarmed step back and Carrie stepped forward, the knife held high. She was smiling. She brought the knife down in an arc and plunged it into the base of the waitress' throat. Then Carrie stepped quickly to the side.

The waitress pinwheeled her arms and stumbled back, but Carrie grabbed one thrashing arm and pulled her forward, into the darkness of the alley. The waitress made a hissing, mewling sound that seemed more to seep from around the knife than to come from her mouth. She reached for the knife. One flailing hand struck it, causing it to sink deeper, slicing as it went. She sank to her knees. Her tears caught hints of light and glinted as they slid down her face. She put her hands on the ground in front of her; it was gritty and slick with the grease the kitchen workers dumped back here. She got her knees under her and started to stand. She understood that she had to get back out into the light. Someone from the kitchen would see her. They would help.

A gentle hand grasped her elbow and helped her up. The waitress turned toward the hand, but there was no one, the hand was gone. Then she felt the hand on her shoulder blade, pushing, turning her gently. She was saved; she was being helped. She acquiesced under the tender touch, relief flowing through her. She stood where the hand positioned her, dazed and in a fog of red pain. She'd already lost enough blood to make her light-headed.

The waitress sensed a claustrophobic closeness of something in front of her. Right at her face. She reached out one trembling hand. Her fingers skated across roughly pitted metal. The dumpster, she was facing the dumpster, but why—

She was shoved rudely from behind and realized a split second before impact that she'd been set up. She'd been turned by her attacker toward the dumpster for this last blow.

The knife connected with the dumpster first and sliced down, buried to its hilt in her neck. Then the waitress' body met the unyielding side of the dumpster and the knife tilted sharply to the right, slicing across and into her jugular, releasing the remainder of her life's blood in a jet.

She rebounded off the dumpster and was dead before she hit the ground.

Carrie knelt next to her and tried to pull the knife from her throat. She pulled and pulled, but it seemed stuck on something, each pull merely shaking the waitress' body. Finally, she rose up and placed her foot on the waitress' neck for leverage. With both hands on the knife she yanked and finally it sprang free. She was quick to jump back and away from the last few gushes. So far, she'd gotten none of the waitress' blood on her and she wanted to keep it that way. She was too fond of her out-fit to let the waitress ruin it.

She wiped the knife handle with the tail of the wait-ress' blouse. Then, keeping the cloth around the handle, she stuck the knife deep into the waitress' stomach, be-cause she couldn't reach her neck again without getting fresh prints on the knife.

It never occurred to Carrie to wonder why she just didn't leave the knife on the ground or even toss it into the dumpster. Perhaps she just liked the stabbing part.

She stood and started down the alley, never glancing back. She didn't need to; she'd taken care of that piece of business.

Now on to her next one.

That whore receptionist.

* * *

"Where was it you wanted me to let you off, Mark?"

The Devil looked left and right as they rode slowly down Nassau Street. The driver, Bill, had told the Devil that Nassau was more or less the main drag through Princeton. Now the Devil was hoping some instinct would push him in the right direction. But it didn't seem as though that was going to be the case. Unease bit at him like swarming piranha, nibbling away at his equilibrium. He felt pushed and it was making him angry.

"Here," he said, and resigned himself to more walking, more searching.

"Right here?" Bill asked. His voice was startled. "But, this is…are you sure this is where you wanted to go?"

"Yes."

"Cause it sounds sort of…well…random. Sounds like you just now decided."

"I did."

"Well listen, Mark, you can get out here or I can take you further, it's all the same to me! But I thought you knew where you were going."

"Yes, here. This is where I was going. Now, stop the car." A growl of irritation slipped into his voice and he turned his flat gaze on the driver.

The skin on Bill's neck tightened.

"Uh, sure, sure thing. You got it, Mark. No problem."

Bill Bixby drove away with a sharp sense of relief. He liked most people and that's why he picked up the occasional hitchhiker, but something about that guy…he had seemed off. Bill couldn't put his finger on how, exactly, but he did feel as though–right at the end there–he'd stumbled into a big pile of sleeping snakes. He was just as glad to get the guy (and his cat) behind him.

It was better than six months before he picked up another hitcher.

The Devil stood with Sitri sitting at his feet. Becoming a cat had done wonders for Sitri's attitude, actually. He hadn't complained once in the past two hours.

The Devil flipped open his phone to check the time. 6:25 A.M. Traffic was very light. Dawn was coming on, but most people still had their headlights lit. He glanced behind him. Alden Brother's Brewery. A sliver of unease whispered into his mind. He squinted up at the sign and then back to the front door, the windows. He shook his head. He did not know this place.

A hiss from his left caught his attention. A mangy orange cat stood at the edge of the alley with its ears back and body close to the ground. Its green eyes were fixed on Sitri. Sitri hissed back and then looked at the Devil, eyes wide and startled, almost as if asking why he'd done that. The orange cat hissed again and now Sitri charged, yowling, a line of fur raised down his back.

"Sitri, control yourself!" the Devil said, but to no avail. Sitri's tail was disappearing around the corner. The devil followed him into the alley.

"Sitri," the Devil said, his own voice now a hiss. He was

too aware of the early hour and the many, many windows in the building next to him. He was halfway down the alley, trying to see Sitri in the first light. "Sitri! Come back or I'll be forced to—"

The orange cat burst from behind a row of trashcans and ran past the Devil, headed to the street. The Devil turned and followed him with his eyes. The cat hit the sidewalk at the end of the alley and darted left and out of his sight.

At that moment, Kelly drove past.

The Devil stood in shock and then pounded up the alley, stumbling twice in his urgency. He skidded out onto the sidewalk, already turned in the direction she'd been going. She was gone. He closed his hands into fists.

A driver coming the opposite direction saw a man with hotly glowing orange eyes and he braked hard, spilling his coffee and yelping at the painful heat as it soaked his crotch. He looked up from the mess in his lap and now the man was just a man standing on the sidewalk, hands rolled into fists. Guy looked pissed, but not fire from your eyes pissed. Must have been the sun. The driver shuddered and drove on. He wouldn't admit to himself that the sun wasn't that far up yet. Not high enough to make someone's eyes look like the burning pits of Hell. He laughed a little, but it was shaky. He'd have to go back home and change. Maybe he just wouldn't go in at all today. In fact, he suddenly felt like spending some extra time with his wife.

Sitri walked low and shame-faced from the mouth of the alley. The Devil controlled an urge to kick his scrawny body into the brick wall behind them.

"She can't be far. She must have turned at the next light. Let's go."

The Devil trotted in the direction Kelly had gone, Sitri running gracefully beside him.

* * *

Carrie had gone back to the offices of Thomas Evigan after…well, after she'd taken care of the waitress. She'd tried the windows and doors, but everything was locked up tight. Although this office might still resemble the charming old house it had once been, the small, pulsing red lights in the corners alerted Carrie to the sophisticated alarm system that protected it.

She could wait.

She was good at biding her time.

She called a cab company advertised on a bus bench and when the cab arrived, she asked him to take her to the nearest hotel.

"Not one of those hoity-toity Bed and Bread places, either. I mean a regular hotel."

"No Bed and Bread for you, huh?" the cabbie said and grinned at her in the rearview mirror, thinking she'd laugh at her own mistake once she'd heard it repeated back to her.

He met her eyes in the mirror and she stared at him blankly. Her eyes glittered coldly with each passing streetlight.

"No, no Bed and Bread. Like I just told you. Just a regular hotel." She didn't like his grin, his teasing tone.

"Yeah, I heard you," the Cabbie said. "It's just that…it's called a Bed and Breakfast…not Bread; Breakfast. It was just funny." His tone was light and friendly, inviting her to laugh.

Carrie didn't laugh.

She leaned forward abruptly, her face nearly pressed to the dividing glass.

"How about you shut the fuck up and go fuck yourself. Is that funny, too?"

She sat back, looking out the side window.

The cabbie felt as though ice water had been dumped over his head. He said no more and drove her to a run-down dive of a motel at the edge of the township–the Red Devil Motor Court. It advertised 'CABEL IN EVRY ROOM' and 'POOL' 'POOL CLOSED' and 'TRUKERS WELCOME!!'

He'd had to go farther to get to this particular one, but

he figured when she saw it and got upset, then he could tell her to go fuck herself. He'd only taken her where she'd wanted to go. And if she gave him shit about the fare then he'd call the cops. He wouldn't hesitate.

But she exited the cab without a word. He told her the fare and she passed it through the window, unconcernedly. Along with a tip. She didn't even spare him a glance. It was almost as though the entire incident hadn't happened.

He leaned over as she was walking to the office. Contrarily, he said:

"Hey, lady, you sure you want to stay here? This one's kind of…kind of rough."

She stopped and turned.

"Honey, they ain't even seen rough till they seen me." Her tone was flirtatious and bawdy and somehow older, like a forty-five-year-old dance hall girl ready to take over as the Madam. She pursed her lips in a kiss.

The cabbie nodded and shot her a half grin, but his stomach turned in disgust. He sat back and powered the window up, glad to have her out of his cab. What a weird little bitch, he thought.

Carrie was not troubled by the flickering neon, the bug encrusted lightbulbs over each door, the dirt lot, the grunts coming from the half open door to one of the rooms, or the ape behind the counter with the crawling eyes.

"Sooooo, pig!" he said, admiration lighting up his features. If his eyes could have detached themselves, they'd already be rolling across the dusty floor to try and climb into her blouse. "Yer a dolly, there, little gal!" He nodded, seemingly in agreement with himself.

Carrie smiled briefly.

"Got a room for me, stud?"

The clerk's hands went to his chest, unconsciously massaging his own hanging boobs. He flushed bright red.

"You know I do, little gal, you know I got something for you!" He honked out a laugh. In his excitement, he pulled one of his boobs right out the arm of his wife-beater t-shirt. It hung, hairy and pendulous and quivering at his manipulations.

"Just the room would be fine." Carrie said.

The clerk sat down, deflated.

"Sure, uh…license, and…I need your license, and…" He rubbed his greasy black hair, trying to massage his thoughts into place. His lips were full, too full, and slick with spit. He looked like a drooler, for sure. "And sixty bucks." He finished in triumph and smiled at her. He raised his arm behind him to grab a key from the rack and a waft of body odor, both oniony and vinegary, assailed her.

She blinked. Then she smiled again.

"I don't have a license, sweetheart, we'll have to do without that. Would forty be good for the room?"

"Uuuh." He stared at her, his mouth hanging open. Then he shook his head. "Uh…no…I always gotta get a license. Got to. It's, uh, it's policy." He continued to shake his head. One hand snuck back to his boob and massaged meditatively.

Carrie smiled and leaned on the counter, pushing her boobs into the v of her vest.

"Maybe we can work something out." She said. She smiled at the clerk.

"Uh, sure. Sure thing. Course we can! What did you have in mind?"

She reached over the counter and put her hand flat in his lap. His chinos were somewhat damp. He tensed and honked out his laugh again. She pressed down. She could feel the outline of his dick. It was small, but growing. She pressed harder and twisted her hand. She was about to offer a blowjob when suddenly the area under her hand got much, much hotter. He had come.

His eyes fluttered and he grunted.

"Okay," he said. "Okay, no license." His gargled the words. "I still gotta charge you the sixty, though; this ain't my place and the owner, he's really—"

"No problem," she said. "There's just one more little thing…" she leaned over and whispered in his ear. His eyelids fluttered again as if fanned by her breath. Then she dropped a hundred and sixty dollars on the counter and grabbed the key. She disappeared through the door.

It took him a while to recover. He slid the three twenties into the safe box and the rest into his pocket. Then he shuffled to the small bathroom at the back. He stuffed a wad of toilet paper down the front of his chinos. He didn't want to have to wash these pants; they were his work ones and he had another shift here tomorrow.

Carrie lay on the bed, on her back, on top of the covers. She lay in the dark, her eyes glittering coldly, though there was no light in the room. She didn't think; her brain merely droned along in a blank neutral. She knew the clerk would leave her 'gift' some time during the night, after his shift had ended. She didn't have to worry about staying awake to greet him; he had a key, after all. She felt very much at home here, as a matter of fact.

After a while she closed her eyes and slept.

* * *

The Devil turned the corner at the light but saw no sign of Kelly's car. He trotted three more blocks, looking left and right, but something just felt off. The trail felt cold this way. He stopped and stood still, hands on his hips. He considered his options.

If she had come down this road, then she could easily be long gone by now. There were too many streets to search. He should just pick up where he'd left off, focusing his thoughts on the lawyer. He needed to find Thomas Evigan before God, Himself put an end to this quest. And the longer he was here on Earth, the more strongly the Devil felt that God, Himself would be ending it. And soon.

But he couldn't turn his thoughts from Kelly. He could not shake the feeling that he needed to be near her, to protect her, but from what? Even seeing her go past, it had to have been a sign. Didn't it? He had seen her…hadn't he?

Sitri twined around his ankles and the Devil shoved him away with one foot.

"Not now, Sitri, I have to concentrate."

Sitri sat in front of the Devil and stared at him intently, yellow eyes glowing almost as if with internal fire. He raised one paw up, indicating the direction they'd come from.

The Devil shook his head.

"You can't know that, Sitri. She could be anywhere."

Sitri stood and turned in an impatient circle and then sat again. He raised his paw.

The Devil stared at Sitri, his anger and impatience mounting. Either way, he was wasting time; he felt it like carelessly spent money from the pockets of a miser.

He sighed sharply and looked over his shoulder at the mostly empty road, in the direction he assumed she'd gone. Then he looked back they way they'd come; the way Sitri wanted to go. He shook his head with frustration and looked at Sitri.

"Okay, let's go."

* * *

Thomas Evigan pulled into his usual spot. He smiled his customary, self-satisfied smile as he gazed at his building, but the smile faded quickly, leaving an unsure blankness on his features. He should have felt great, and he tried to tell himself that he did feel great…but he didn't.

The truth was, he still felt shaken from last night.

Kelly's car was in the lot. That helped set his mind at ease. Everything in its place, after all. He chuckled, but that died, too.

He exited his car and leaned against it, allowing the unease to run its course. That little bitch and her ridiculous, psychopathic nature had ruined his equilibrium. Thomas had been around long enough to know that this, too, would pass; that he'd get to work and get to feeling better, but what if she came back? She had seemed cowed last night, but she hadn't seemed…genuine. Had he re-

ally intimidated her or was it merely part of her reper-
toire?

And how could he ever know the difference?

He shook his head and pushed himself away from the
car. Maybe he wouldn't know unless she showed up
again. Like a mold stain through cheap paint.

He entered the office, looking to his right, to where
Kelly would be. A manufactured smile was spreading
across his features.

"Good morning, Kelly, I hope—"

He saw everything in rapid-fire, like shutter clicks of a
good camera. Each piece of information burst on his
brain like a flash:

Kelly was at her desk.

Carrie was behind her.

Carrie had a knife to Kelly's throat.

Carrie's other hand was hidden behind Kelly's back.

Carrie was smiling.

"Hello, Lover," she said. Her voice was soft and breathy;
Marilyn Monroe again. She wore the same clothes she'd
had on last night, but now they were disheveled. Her
knees were dirty and some of the lace had split at the
seam exposing her leg and allowing the denim to gap and
gather bunchily. The boots were dirty and the heels had
a ragged look where the pleather was peeling up. Her
hair was in a shambles.

"Are you surprised to see me?" She tilted her head and batted her lashes at him.

He nodded, unable to speak. Unable to take his eyes from the knife at Kelly's throat. He was thinking: is she going to turn that knife on me? oh no, no no no…I can't allow that!

"I thought you'd be surprised," she said. "Your secretary certainly was. Weren't you, hon?" She pressed the knife harder against Kelly's throat. Kelly made no reply but her fingers curled around the arms of her chair and she swallowed visibly. Her eyes never left Thomas.

"Yes, your whore secretary was very surprised to see me. Didn't you tell her about us, Thomas? Didn't you tell her that her…services…weren't going to be needed any longer?"

He shook his head, whether he was in denial of what she said or just in denial of the entire situation was unclear.

"Speak, Thomas, speak!" she said. "I command it!" Then she laughed. "You really thought you had me last night, didn't you? Really thought you'd put me in my place, right? Well guess what, lover? My place is right next to you. And just as soon as I take out the trash, then everything begins for us. It took you a long time to come for me, but you did it in the end, didn't you? You came for me and here I am. And I will never leave you. But you can't fuck around on me, Thomas. I can't have that. A dead Thomas is better than a cheating Thomas." Now she showed him the hand that had been behind Kelly's back. She was holding the gun that the clerk from the motel had secured for her.

Thomas had been shaking his head through her entire speech. When he saw the gun, he knew he had no choice in his actions. He plunged.

"I never messed around with her, Carrie. She wanted to, yes, she is always coming on to me…but I never once…I mean, look at her…she's got nothing on you…"

Kelly's eyes had gone wide as her mouth dropped open. She stared at Thomas in disbelief.

"No," she said, her voice barely above a whisper. "It's not true, none of it is true—"

"Shut up, Kelly, for God's sake, just give it up! You think Carrie is a dumb hick, but she's not and she's got you figured out. Everything you told me yesterday…" his eyes cut from Kelly to Carrie to see how this was going over. "…about how you thought she looked like a real bitch and you put something in her water, trying to make her look like a fool…"

Carrie's eyes were shining. This was it at last, the kind of love she deserved. She knew there had been something wrong with that water. No one in their right mind would drink that shit on purpose.

"I realize it now, Carrie, I see it all. We're so right for each other. Could you possibly love me as much as I love you? Oh Carrie, I so want for us to be together."

"I do too, Thomas! It's everything I want!"

"God, that makes me so happy." He took a step toward her, smiling, but then he let the smile fall from his face. He considered his next manipulation. He had to handle it just right to give himself time to call the cops. Thomas didn't want Carrie to kill Kelly–not in his offices–but more than that, he didn't want Carrie to kill him. "But it's hopeless," he said. He let his shoulders slump and lowered his head dramatically.

Carrie hesitated at Kelly's side, the knife dropping away. Thomas saw her indecision. She was thinking of running to him. Leaving Kelly the opportunity to break free. He couldn't have that!

He stood straight and threw out his arm, his finger pointing shakily at Kelly. He forced outrage into his voice and manufactured a break at the end.

"We can't be together because of her!"

"What do you mean, Thomas?" Carrie cried and remembered to hold the knife tight to Kelly's throat. Kelly shook her head, no, no, no, but Carrie stilled it with a press of the knife.

"Because she knows things, she can blackmail me. I didn't want to tell you any of this, I feel like such a…such a…fool." He faked a tone of utter despair. Then he looked into Carrie's eyes. "Only you can help me, Carrie. I know you can make this right. I don't know what you want to do. I realize you must be very angry with Kelly, and I wouldn't blame you! After everything…"

Carrie was still staring at him and her eyes shone like that of a feral animal considering injured prey.

"Carrie, darling, no one would blame you for…for making this right. This woman is trying to stop me…stop us! From getting everything we deserve. It's not right. Anyone could see that."

Carrie was nodding, pushing the blade edge further into Kelly's throat. A thin line of blood appeared under the knife.

Carrie stowed the gun in the pocket of her jeans and motioned Kelly up. Kelly was weak in the knees and she fell back a bit as she tried to stand. Carrie shoved her roughly forward, tilting the chair over onto the floor. She tugged Kelly's purse over her own shoulder.

"Let's go," she said. Then she addressed Thomas. "I know where to take her. They won't notice anything at that shithole. I know how to fix this. Just wait for me, darling."

She motioned Kelly toward the door. When they were even with Thomas, Carrie tilted her head to him, closed her eyes and parted her lips.

Thomas could see the hot red slug of her tongue moving slickly in the dark cave of her mouth. Her breath was atrocious, deadly. He leaned forward, holding his breath. His lips met hers. He was kissing the monster.

Her mouth parted more and her tongue pushed into his mouth and he felt the glob of spit it brought with it. He nearly gagged but knew if he did, he'd be dead. Better Kelly than me, better Kelly than me, he repeated in his head. It calmed his gag reflex.

Carrie pulled away, her eyelids half lowered. She ran the back of her hand across her mouth and a runner of saliva trailed like a silvery string from her chin to her hand until it broke off and disappeared.

"I'll be back," she said, her voice husky. "Wait for me, lover."

Thomas nodded and used all his strength to pull a smile onto his face. He never looked at Kelly.

As the door closed behind them, he let out a pent up breath and leaned dizzily over his knees. He heard Kelly's car start. He listened as it backed down the gravel drive. Feeling his stomach twist, he ran to the small guest bath behind the stairs and vomited.

He knew he should call the police right away. He'd be able to give them the description of Kelly's car and they'd jump if he said jump. The police would have that crazy bitch rounded up in no time.

But what about Kelly? She'd tell everyone about his betrayal of her. He knew she couldn't be bought, it was one of the reasons he'd hired her himself. Her innate honesty, her goodness, showed in everything she did.

The press would crucify him.

He could always say he fainted. He'd give it a half hour or so, maybe an hour, enough time for that crazy bitch to do...whatever she was going to do. If Kelly wasn't dead when the police found them, then he'd take that as a sign that she was meant to live and he was meant to be found out. Maybe he'd wait ninety minutes. How long does a faint usually last?

He straightened with difficulty and leaned over the sink, groaning.

He splashed cold water on his face and stood, reaching blindly for the little hand towel. He dried his face and looked into the mirror.

A man was standing right behind him.

* * *

The Devil had been a block away when he'd seen Kelly's car backing out of a driveway beside a large Victorian. His heart had filled with a joy he'd not known since he'd been Lucifer, happy in Heaven. He sprinted.

He was twenty feet from the car as she turned out into

the street away from him. She saw him, he knew she did, but her eyes were wide and terror-stricken. As she put the car back into drive, he saw the knife at her throat. Her eye rolled back to him, demonstrating her desperate unhappiness.

Then she nodded, deliberately indicating the building she'd just left. Her tires shrieked as she sped off. From behind, the Devil saw the other person in the car, but he couldn't tell who it was.

His body tensed to run after her. He knew he couldn't catch a speeding car, but maybe he could. If he really pushed this body. He felt a pinprick, like a needle, in the back of his leg. He turned in fury but Sitri had already sprung away. Now he trotted, tail switching, to the side door of the Victorian.

After one more glance down the now empty street, the Devil followed Sitri up the drive.

He pushed open the door and glanced around. There were some small signs of a struggle: the pencil and pen cup had scattered its contents across the desk; a vase had been upended, and a chair at the small reception desk had been overturned.

Sitri pushed past him and further into the room. He hesitated for one brief second and then trotted down the main hallway where he turned and stared intently at a half closed door.

The Devil came forward and listened to the sounds of splashing water. Who would be washing their face during an assault and kidnapping? He tented his fingers on the door and pushed it silently inward. He saw a figure huddled over the sink.

The figure straightened, wiping his face on a small towel and then dropped it carelessly to the floor. He met the Devil's eyes in the mirror.

"Hello, Thomas," the Devil said. "I've been looking for you."

Christine Dougherty

BOOK FIVE

The Devil's Judgment

Thomas turned quickly, his back connecting with the sink in the tight space. Three things occurred to him simultaneously: did he know this guy, could he take him in a fight, and what the fuck was a cat doing in his office. He hated cats. All animals, really.

"Who the fuck are you?" He meant it to come out as a challenge, a warning, but he found he was barely able to squeak it out. His knees were shaking. His stomach was shaking. He felt his hands begin to shake and he reached behind him to grip the smooth, cool edge of the porcelain sink. That grounded him a bit and stopped the vertigo that had been trying to creep over him.

The Devil shook his head. He was at a crossroads. The man he'd come to judge was right here in front of him, but Kelly was in danger, and obviously, Evigan knew something about it. He could take him to Hell and be done, be back where he belonged. Possibly that course would even lessen the amount of punishment that God, Himself might decide the Devil deserved for his transgression. It would be the easier and certainly more satisfying choice—he ached with the need to judge this man.

But then, what of Kelly? He'd felt the mortal danger

she was in. But if she were to be killed, she would go to Heaven and dwell forever in Paradise. She was an Innocent.

That thought did not comfort him.

He decided.

"Who has Kelly?"

"Who the fuck are you?" Thomas said again, and this time, his voice did rise. Rage swept into the Devil like an inferno, lighting his eyes and trying to push reason out a back door.

The Devil reached out and Thomas shrank back against the sink. He had to be hallucinating or maybe he really had passed out after throwing up, because it looked like this guy's eyes were on fire. And that simply was not possible.

The Devil's hands grasped Thomas' arms and he pulled him close; they were almost nose to nose. Thomas could feel the heat of those terrible, burning eyes on his face. It was not a good heat, one that warmed your joints and soothed and comforted—no—this heat was somehow painful in a way that induced instant nausea. He felt his lower belly rumble and then clamp as though diarrhea was imminent. His skin seemed to dry and shrink, making it hard even to blink his desert-parched eyes, and the smell was worse. It did not seem to come from the man's mouth; his mouth was closed. Somehow, the stench was coming from his eyes; it was part and parcel with the heat.

Thomas thought of the enormous, fly-blown deer that had greeted him and three friends when they'd gone to a lake cabin one year to fish. The deer carcass had been about twenty feet from the cabin, right near the driveway. They'd smelled it even as they'd left the road and it had been with them the entire week—the carcass was much too deteriorated to even contemplate moving. They'd have needed snow shovels.

When he'd gotten home, Thomas had thrown away every piece of clothing he'd brought with him on that trip. It seemed the smell clung in a way that mere washing would never be able to clean away.

"Thomas," the man said, "I am the Devil."

When the Devil had revealed himself to Kelly, she hadn't believed; nothing in her life would ever have led her to believe that she'd have occasion to consort with the Devil. Thomas, however…he believed immediately. Almost as though he'd been expecting it.

"What…what do you want? My soul? You can have it! I don't care…take it!"

From another human, this invitation might have spun the Devil into a dizzied frenzy—to be offered a soul? It was like waving a juicy steak before a raging carnivore.

Thomas, however, didn't believe he had a soul. He believed in the Devil, if only because he'd long thought to himself that if (big if) there was a Hell that he'd surely be going. But Thomas didn't believe in souls, or rather, he thought that if there was a soul in him, he could most likely do without it.

"Listen carefully, Thomas," the Devil said. "Who took Kelly? Where did they take her?"

Thomas shook his head. Why was the Devil concerned with Kelly? Could it be that she was his target, not him? Or possibly Carrie? Yes! That had to be it! She'd killed her own kid for Christ's sake! Of course the Devil was here for her! Burgeoning relief was accreting up through his body. He just had to give Carrie up? No problem! Then his mind whispered to him: she is guilty, yes, but so too, aren't you?

Fuck you, mind, he thought back. What am I guilty of? Doing my job?

"It was Carrie. Carrie Walsh, she killed her own kid. It was disgusting. She's some kind of psychopath and you should…"

The Devil had pulled back slightly at the name 'Carrie Walsh', giving Thomas the impression that he'd been correct, this Devil was here for Carrie. But he seemed almost startled or shocked, as though he'd had no idea that Carrie was nearby. Something clicked and Thomas realized…the Devil was looking for Kelly and there was a certain desperation in his eyes, one that Thomas had seen a thousand times before.

The Devil loved Kelly? Could that be right? Thomas thought so, yes.

"Where has she taken Kelly?" the Devil growled into his face, gripping his arms even tighter.

Thomas' mind was in a cold whirl of calculation.

"Why do you want to know?" he asked, his voice taking on a slightly belligerent tone.

He expected the Devil before him to fly into a rage. He was ready for a furious tirade against him, but, his mind had calculated, the Devil wouldn't hurt him as long as he had information the Devil needed.

But the Devil only smiled as the fire left his eyes. It sent a ripple of fresh fear through Thomas the way a rage might not have. The Devil dropped Thomas' arms and leaned against the wall across from the sink. He crossed his arms over his chest.

"Have a seat, my dear," the Devil said, indicating the toilet. Sitri twined around Thomas' legs as he shuffled to the right, nearly tripping him. Once Thomas was seated, Sitri leaped nimbly to the sink and perched on its edge. He looked from the Devil to Thomas with grim expectation, as if this were a highly anticipated sporting event of uneven odds.

Which, in a way, it was. Even Thomas knew that.

"Terms," the Devil said.

"Huh?"

"Your terms, Thomas, for giving me the information to save an innocent woman's life. What are your terms?"

Thomas was nodding even before the Devil finished. It was as he thought. They were bargaining. He felt a swaggering, boastful sense of confidence–he could bargain with the best of them. Ego alone kept him from realizing he was dealing with the Devil, but he could hardly be held to fault for that. Ego had tripped up greater men than he.

"Okay, uh…my terms."Thomas had a bargaining strategy that had served him very well. It was unexpected, and it generally gave him an advantage over his opponent: he asked the outrageous first. "President of the United States. That's what I want. And um, let's see…a wife. One who has money of her own. Beautiful, but not bright, not ambitious. Like a Stepford wife…you familiar with that movie? That's what I want. Oh, and I want to live well into my nineties without discomfort. And when I do die, I want to go in my sleep. And never gain weight, that's important, too…and not get wrinkly…and my hair can't go completely gray…and my wife shouldn't lose her figure even after kids…and um…let me think…"

Thomas had hunched over, his chin in his hand, thinking hard. Rodin would have recognized him.

"I guess uh…just, you know, perfection. That's what I'm talking about. A perfect life where I get everything I deserve. Everything. Got it?" He looked up at the Devil. His voice had strengthened as he'd listed the components of his perfect life, but when he turned to look to see if the Devil was getting all this, his voice faltered.

The Devil had not changed position, nor had his familiar. The Devil was smiling. A cynical, weary twist of his lips. Something small and long-buried in Thomas tried to worm its way into his consciousness…some deep and ancient part of his brain was trying to sound an alarm, the part that felt compelled to throw rocks at the sun or huddle in terror when thunder crashed incomprehensibly through the skies.

He quashed that part, thinking of it only as cowardly.

"Well?" he asked, forcing belligerence into his tone. "You got it or what?"

The Devil's smile widened a few degrees more and he nodded once.

"Thomas Evigan, we have a deal." His tone was mild and he put his hand out, but Thomas shook his head, drawing back. He didn't want to feel that heat or be assaulted again by that stench.

"Uh, no, thanks, we don't have to shake on it. I'll just take you at your word; how's that?"

"As you wish." The Devil nodded again. "Now. Where has Carrie taken Kelly?"

"Well, listen," Thomas stood and edged past the cat on the sink and slid out the bathroom door. He was careful not to make eye contact with the Devil. "Let's get my car, and we'll head in the direction they went." He was patting his pockets. "Keys, keys…oh, here they are…we'll head in the direction they went. Carrie had to have stayed locally last night, and she mentioned…well, let's start out and we'll go from there." He finished cagily, feeling the weight of the Devil following close behind.

A heavy hand dropped to his shoulder.

"Thomas." The Devil's voice was flat. Ominous. Thomas stopped his frantic movements and stood still, listening. The cat twined around his legs as though he were the embodiment of the Devil's voice.

"Yes?" Thomas said, trying to keep his own voice as neutral as possible. Still, a small quaver shook the one word he spoke.

"If we don't find Kelly alive and unhurt…" the hand squeezed, sending fingers of heat needling into the muscles of his shoulder and back. "The deal is off."

Thomas swallowed, feeling the heat nearing his heart and throat, drawing a line of sweat across his upper lip. He nodded. The hand slid from his shoulder. The sinking heat disappeared immediately.

The sweat remained, a salty reminder of the nearness of Hell.

* * *

Carrie had sunk back in the passenger seat, but she kept her head turned toward Kelly. She still held the knife, but had transferred the gun to Kelly's purse, which she had tucked between her boots for safe-keeping. You can't carry your purse on your lap–that was practically an invitation to get your ass car-jacked.

"I can't believe you thought you could get him," Carrie said. She shook her head, mouth twisted into a disgusted, incredulous sneer. "I mean, have you ever looked at yourself? You're like, butt-fucking ugly." Her eyes traveled over Kelly's plain white blouse and sensible cotton skirt. "And you dress like a fucking nun. Nobody wants that shit, man." She snorted laughter. She raised one booted leg nimbly to the dashboard. "This is what they want. You think I like these boots? Guess the fuck again, be-cause I don't. These are for men–for Thomas, I mean, but they all want this shit; they're all dirty pigs. Think they can suck your tits forever. Whole world wants them to suck your tits." She sighed. She was looking at the ru-ined toe of the boot on the dash and her voice had dropped. She was sulking. "They're all just a bunch of animals, the women, too. They act like they're not...act like they're special...fucking whores and bitches, all of them." She looked at Kelly. "You too, I can tell. You especially!" Now her voice was climbing to a higher register. "How could you think you'd take him from me?"

Kelly did not dare glance at Carrie. She was trying to follow the girl's train of thought, trying to find an in...a way toward conversation...but Carrie was so disjointed, and so volatile!

But Carrie still stared at her, seemingly expecting an answer. Kelly cleared her throat. She felt the tug of the shallow cut Carrie's knife had put there.

"I didn't...I didn't know..."

"LIAR!" Carrie screamed, lunging across the seats. The car jerked as Kelly's arms tensed for a blow and she cried out. But Carrie sat back, laughing.

"Scared ya, right?" She laughed again. Kelly felt dazed; punched out and staggering. She glanced to her right. Now Carrie was staring out the window, humming.

Kelly knew she was in deep trouble. She knew she had to try and keep her head if she was to have a chance. Her thoughts went to the Devil. Ambivalent as she felt about him, she still wished he were here. She would have liked to see him again. Before...before anything happened. She thought about her parents, too. How they might have to face losing both their children. That thought encouraged her to try again.

"Carrie, I didn't…" she paused, seeing Carrie turn toward her. "I didn't know that you loved Thomas. I didn't even know you before yesterday, can't you see that?" She kept her tone reasonable and calm.

"Thomas never mentioned me before," Carrie said, an edge creeping back into her voice. "Is that what you're trying to tell me? That I'm just not very important?"

Carrie continued to watch her. Kelly felt she was walking a tightrope over a moat populated with nightmare beasts ready to leap. She thought hard.

"I wouldn't try to keep you and Thomas apart," she said. "I would never do that."

"No, I know you won't keep us apart," Carrie said. Her voice was flat. "I'm going to make sure of it."

A twist of frustration tried to work its way into Kelly's stomach at Carrie's deliberate misunderstanding, but she fought it down, maintaining her outward calm. She wouldn't get anywhere if she fought with Carrie.

She had to find an avenue to her. And she had to find it fast.

Kelly shifted in her seat and Carrie's head snapped in her direction. Kelly could see Carrie taking a breath to say something, but she spoke over her.

"Carrie, how do you know Thomas?" Her voice was casually inquisitive. They could have been two girls chatting at a cocktail reception, just getting to know each other.

Carrie's mouth closed and opened again. She turned away from Kelly then turned back. She seemed torn by some inner mayhem.

"He saved me. Saved my life," she said finally. Her voice was that of a very young girl. Kelly glanced at Carrie in surprise and then masked it by glancing at the rear view mirror.

"That's…that's amazing," Kelly said. "That's why you love him so much." She saw Carrie nod in her peripheral vision. Her head was down and she toyed distractedly with the knife in her lap.

"Yeah. He's my hero." Carrie sighed and Kelly felt it again: the sense that there were many, many people packed into Carrie's body. Or, more to the point, many personas. But Carrie wore her guises clumsily, sloppily. It was easy to see behind her makeshift facades once you'd spent any length of time with her.

"How did he save your life?" Kelly's kept her voice calm but interested. Slightly admiring. She knew instinctively not to lay it on thick…Carrie would spot that as easily as a thief spots the flaw in his own shaky defenses.

Carrie didn't say anything for a minute or two, but Kelly waited patiently. She knew that Carrie was constructing. Creating what she would say next.

"I was…I was accused of a terrible crime…" Carrie's voice was soft, hesitant. The voice of someone reluctantly recalling a difficult time. She didn't want to talk about it, her voice intimated, but she would if she had to…strictly as a favor to her listener…

"Some people were out to get me, and they framed me. Said I committed this really horrible…that I had murdered…someone, and the police, well, I think it might actually have been the police who framed me. And the prosecutor. He framed me, too. Said a bunch of things that weren't true at all. Perjured himself actually. I think…" Carrie's eyes had a far-away quality as she fabricated another new past for herself. "I think probably the prosecutor was in love with me, but I had turned him away. I didn't want anything to do with him. So he framed me. It was horrible. Really, I was in a fight for my life and no one was on my side. Even my parents weren't on my side. But then Thomas showed up like an angel from heaven, you know? Christ, it was like he'd been put on this earth just to protect me! And we fell in love right away. Of course." She gave Kelly a shy little half-smile. "We're here."

Kelly had been trying to follow the thread of Carrie's story, but there was nothing to follow. She was a bundle of wishes and delusions incapable of truth. But when she said "we're here" Kelly was caught off-guard, trying to piece it into the rest of Carrie's narrative.

She shook her head.

"We're here?"

"Yeah. Turn right into that parking lot. We're here."

The motel was a run-down, one story u shaped building with parking in the center courtyard area. Catching sight of the sign—Red Devil Motor Court—Kelly felt another ache of regret that she might never see the Devil again. She realized she no longer thought of him as her brother…that familial nostalgia couldn't be what made her wish she could see him just one more time. Did she love him? Yes, she was pretty sure she did, but it wasn't the yearning, infatuated, sexually charged love you felt at a new relationship—it was the ingrained, time-tested, unquestioned love you have for someone who seems to have always been in your life; whose presence you never question. The kind of love so solidified that you never even had to mention it. It was as much a part of you as your breath and though as little considered, just as sustaining.

She turned into the lot, staring at the sign. The leering, jeering devil face with its fire-engine red horns and nastily lolling forked tongue had nothing whatever to do with her Devil.

Carrie directed her to a space in front of room 215 and Kelly parked. She waited, hands on the steering wheel to see what came next. There was movement in her peripheral vision; Carrie was shaking her head. Harsh sun shone in on her side, highlighting her features. She stared straight out the front window. She looked exhausted.

"You know, I know you're just trying to suck up to me, keep me talking about Thomas." For the first time, Carrie's voice held no particular inflection. There was nothing false in her tone or manner. She was like an actor who has just come off stage from the last show of a play that had had a very long run. "I know why, too. Don't think I don't." She turned her face to Kelly and Kelly shrunk back from Carrie's glittering, yet somehow dead, eyes. "That waitress last night," Carrie continued, confusing Kelly again. "She probably didn't deserve to die. She didn't do anything so bad, I mean, nothing like flirting with Thomas or anything like that." She glittered sharply at Kelly again. "But I killed her anyway. Do you know why? Kelly, do you know why I killed that waitress? Do you know why I killed that neighbor that kept complaining about my dog shitting in her yard and that bitch from the park who told me to stop cursing and there was that teenager that was throwing rocks…and my kid…" Her voice trailed away and she looked down and at first Kelly thought it was from shame, but no; Carrie was merely counting them out on her hand. "Yes, that's right–my son, the teenager, the woman from the park, my neighbor, the waitress…that's five…" She glanced at Kelly, fingers spread wide. "Do you know why I killed each of them? Because they were bugging me. In one way or another, they were being pains in my ass." She yawned, putting the back of her hand to her mouth. "I'm really beat," she said, more or less to herself. "So you see, now, right? Why I killed them?" She looked at Kelly, eyebrows raised. "You see how they were being pains in my ass? Just like you're being?"

Kelly stared, open mouthed and dumbfounded, unable to respond.

Carrie smiled and though it was a thin smile, there was still a hint of genuineness about it. "That's okay, you don't have to answer. I can see in your face that you're sorry. I get that, I really do. Let's…let's get a room and we'll talk some more." A cold amusement had slipped into her voice and coldly glittering eyes. "We'll get it worked out."

Carrie turned and flipped up her door handle but then turned back to Kelly. "We're going to the office together. Don't say a word or I'll kill the clerk, okay?"

Kelly nodded.

"Okay, you can get out now."

Kelly turned and fumbled at her door handle, finally getting it to lift. She felt as though she were moving underwater, the very air having grown dense and unforgiving. It was still early and the traffic on the highway was just beginning to build. Could she make it to the highway? If she ran now?

A hard something pushed into her side and Carrie put her lips to Kelly's ear. She'd gotten around the car so fast! Kelly felt dizzy with fear and disorientation. How did she move so fast in those heels?

"I can read you like a book, honey," Carrie said in her ear and now her voice was the aging whore, the madam, the worldly wise woman who has seen enough to know…well, everything there was to know about the dirty needs of humans. She pressed the pistol more firmly into Kelly's side. "Don't fuck up, honey, you'll be killing lots more than just yourself if you do. Don't forget that."

Kelly nodded and the pistol left her side, but Carrie didn't. She took Kelly's hand. She looked at Kelly shyly from beneath her lashes.

"I never held hands with a girl before," she said, her voice soft and wondering. She giggled. "It feels good," she said and then her face changed again, from wide eyed wonder to smirking flirt. "Does the rest of you feel this good, honey?"

Kelly felt a fresh ripple of fear and then Carrie was pulling her forward, to the office.

* * *

Thomas had balked at letting a cat into his Mercedes. The anguish on his face was as intense as if someone had told him they were going to rape his mother—maybe more so.

"Its nails will go right through the leather!" he said, grief-stricken, as Sitri jumped from the front seat to the back. Sitri didn't even spare him a glance, but he did stretch, tearing ten grooves into the padded back seat. Thomas groaned in despair.

"Get in," the Devil said. He was enjoying the effect Sitri had on Evigan and was glad Sitri had come along. He glanced back to where the cat had stretched itself out across the seat. He thought about giving Sitri a pat on the head, certain the cat part of him would enjoy it, but he was uncertain as to how the Sitri part would react. Probably tear his fingers off. He satisfied himself with a quick nod in Sitri's direction.

The cat winked.

Thomas was bent over his steering wheel, trying to think. She had stayed somewhere overnight, he was certain of that, and it had to be somewhat close by if she had planned all along on coming back this morning. She had said: "they won't notice anything at that shithole"; what shithole did she mean? It couldn't be any of the bed and breakfasts in Princeton proper; they were the antithesis of shitholes.

He felt time slipping through his fingers. He so badly wanted everything the Devil had promised him. So involved was he in the thought of obtaining his fantasies, that it never even occurred to him to wonder what would happen if he couldn't uphold his end of the bargain.

"Which way did they go?" he asked and the Devil pointed down Nassau Street. "Okay, that way leads to Freegate Township; it's a little rougher out there. I think we can find them at one of the motels on 206." Shockingly, he laughed. "At least I hope so! I really want to be President!"

The Devil marveled at the intense self-absorption of this man. He felt the fire of Hell wanting to rise in him, the righteousness of judging this man, the right-ness of it.

A woman ran, screaming, in front of their car.

Thomas braked hard, sending Sitri sliding off the seat and into the wheel well. The Devil threw a hand out, bracing himself against the dashboard.

"Jesus Christ!" Thomas yelled as the woman kept running, almost getting hit by traffic in the opposite lane. Thomas glanced back the way she'd come from. Alden Brother's…where he'd been last night. Another girl stood on the sidewalk, bent double and vomiting. A man was shouting into his cell phone. A strange sort of coldness drew a line up his back as he remembered the way

Carrie had glanced at the waitress. She didn't think he'd seen, but he had. Wouldn't that be weird if…

"Let's go," the Devil said. "We're not going to help them." The Devil knew that what had just occurred was in some way tied to Carrie–he didn't know how he knew, it was just intuition and piecing together the bits and pieces he could gather from Thomas' train of thought.

The Devil couldn't take his eyes from the road ahead of them. The white and yellow lines seemed to glow, rippling and pointing him in the right direction, and he knew he'd find Kelly. But something seemed to be gathering in the air around him, thickening it, and an answering tension was tying his body into cold knots.

He would find Kelly, yes, but would he be in time?

* * *

Carrie pushed Kelly ahead of her into the room. It was dark and Kelly stumbled against the bed, almost falling, but caught herself and stood, looking around.

The clerk hadn't given Carrie any trouble; he'd seemed as mesmerized by her as a stray mongrel panting after a bitch in heat. He'd not even spared Kelly a glance as Carrie had laid the money down in exchange for the key.

Now Carrie turned on the light and turned to the window, making sure the curtains were tight to each other. The room was ugly; there was no other way to say it. It was decorated–if you could use that term–in brown, olive green, and orange that harkened back to the early seventies. In fact, many of the furnishings, bedspread included, had been here since the seventies. And it showed.

There was one lumpy queen bed, one pilly upholstered chair, one dresser with its ornate veneer peeling away, and a tube television so deep that they'd had to build an opening into the wall to accommodate its enormous backside.

The bedspread was a busy swirl of orange and brown with vines of acid green so vibrant that it almost shimmered. It gave Kelly the uneasy impression that it was moving.

Carrie pressed the gun into her lower back.

"Have a seat on the bed, honey," she said. "Let's get some things figured out."

Kelly did as she was told and all the while her mind ran in frantic circles, trying to figure a way out. She didn't think anything she said to Carrie was going to make a difference. Carrie was so far out of her mind that she couldn't even see it with a telescope.

"Scoot your back right up against that headboard, honey, get comfy. I just need to, uh…" Carrie looked at the blank space of the room and then down at herself.

"...this might work."

She wiggled her fingers in under the lace placket where it had split a little from her jeans and tugged. The lace ripped another ten inches down the side. She pulled harder and ripped it right down to her ankle. Then she ripped it clear of the cuff. Now the jeans on her left leg flapped open from her hip to her ankle and when she walked, she flashed a pair of white cotton underwear with a pattern of pink and blue flowers at the waist and leg bands—incongruously innocent, little-girl panties. Then she bent to her right leg and ripped the length of lace from that side, too. Now both legs flared open and she looked as though she wore a wrap skirt but had forgotten half of it.

Coming to the far side of the bed, she told Kelly to put her hands out and she tied her wrists to the post on the headboard. Kelly half sat and half lay, twisted awkwardly. Her hands were pressed together at the level of her shoulders and her legs trailed down the bed. She looked like a praying mermaid.

Carrie drew the chair up to the side of the bed that Kelly faced and she sat, putting her feet on the bed at the bend in Kelly's waist.

"I'm not gonna shoot you," Carrie said and she smiled. "I bet you were worried about that, right? Even ugly chicks don't want to get shot...too fucking messy, right?"

Kelly nodded, tears forming unbidden in her eyes. She clasped her hands and Carrie's eyes went to them. Genuine unease flitted over her features and then was gone. She leaned forward, dropping her feet to the floor and placed her hand on Kelly's breast. She stared into Kelly's eyes.

"This is what they want," she said, her voice confiding as though she were telling Kelly a secret. "They want to suck and suck and suck you…until you're dead." She caressed Kelly's breast through the fabric of her blouse, her hand cupping and lifting it slightly. Kelly's tears overflowed the banks of her lids and coursed freely down her cheeks.

"Carrie," Kelly said, trying to still the tremble in her voice. "Not all of them; they aren't all like that."

Kelly's nipple was pinched roughly and she hissed in a painful breath.

"You don't know, you don't know fucking anything, you want my tits, too? Huh? You fucking whore!" Carrie was standing, screaming, her red face thrust into Kelly's. "You fucking whore! You fucking whore!" Kelly had pulled back as far as her tied hands would allow, but still Carrie came on, leaning over the bed, her hot dragon's breath a nauseating vapor. Kelly shook and tried to hitch in a breath, but her diaphragm seemed locked. The change was so fast, so alarming, it stunned her. She felt as though she'd put her hand in a live socket.

Someone from the next room banged on the wall in frustration. Kelly drew in a breath to call out, but before she could even get the air in her lungs, Carrie had spun away from the bed, hands clenched into fists, her breath whining in and out in harsh gasps as spittle gathered on her lower lip.

"I'LL FUCKING KILL YOU TOO YOU WANT THAT YOU FUCKING SHITHEAP MOTHER-FUCKER YOU WANT ME TO COME THE FUCK OVER THERE?"

She was the picture of rage. The knocker in the other room fell into silence.

Kelly's mind felt wiped clean with terror and she could see nothing, think of nothing, save this creature who seemed made entirely of fury.

Carrie turned and her shoulders dropped, her hands unclenched, and she smiled at Kelly. Her face was still red, but even that was fading to a sallow yellow.

"Did I scare you?" Carrie said. She looked at Kelly with interest. Then she laughed.

Kelly knew there was no reasoning to be done with this monster. She knew she was going to die.

Carrie was back across the room in two strides. When she reached the bed, she didn't stop, she climbed up and crawled across it. Kelly pressed herself back, feeling every bump and knob of the headboard and pulled in a breath to scream. She hadn't wanted to get anyone else hurt or possibly killed, but her terror at this raging demon was too great. Then Carrie was on her, crawling up her, knees on either side of her waist. Carrie loomed over her, hot hands on Kelly's throat and Kelly finally screamed but Carrie's hands pressed and pressed, stopping the scream before it was begun. Slowly but surely, Carrie was cutting off her air. Kelly tried to draw a breath and found she couldn't–the hands at her throat were too tight. She felt as though sharp knives were slicing up through her esophagus and she tasted blood in the back of her throat. She bucked, bringing her legs up, but Carrie hung on. Kelly bucked again, trying to kick and now Carrie was laughing, her eyes glittering wildly, riding her like a mechanical bull. Kelly's throat burned and dots of purest black began to swarm her vision. She jerked her arms reflexively and the lace gave a quarter of an inch. A bloom of hope rose sweetly through the haze forming in Kelly's mind and she yanked her arms again.

In her mind, the lace ripped and she pulled free, rolling Carrie off. She jumped up and ran for the door. It took her forever to get there, but when she did, she dragged it open to blinding white light and she stood, transfixed. She heaved in a deep breath and her throat did not hurt at all, the pain was gone. She looked back into the room, but the room was gone. Carrie was gone. She turned again and now even the door was gone. She turned in a slow circle.

Everything was gone.

Everything was silence and white light.

White light.

White light.

"Hello?" Kelly said.

* * *

The Devil felt a weight settle around him like a lead blanket of despair as Thomas pulled his car in next to Kelly's. Room 215. The Devil knew Kelly was in room 215; he somehow just knew. But he couldn't raise himself from this seat. His limbs felt numb. Too heavy. He lifted one arm toward the door handle. His fingers brushed across it and then dropped. Grayish white haze was filling his mind. Cloudy and cold. Like a heavy fog.

"What's wrong with you?"

The question came to him like a shimmering echo, but flat. Faraway. Unconcerning.

"What the fuck man, are we going in there or not?"

Faraway. Unconcerning.

A hot needle of pain pierced the fog.

The Devil yelled and sat sharply forward, his hand

going to the back of his neck. At the same instant, he had a painful, expelling sensation, like sneezing out an elephant, and then his mind cleared. He twisted and Sitri sat, licking the nails on his left paw. They were extended and wickedly sharp.

Sitri glanced at him, yellow eyes cool and considering, then he raised his gaze to the roof of the car. The Devil followed his gaze.

Christina, the Patron, hovered indistinctly, spread across the headliner like transparent honey. Tears coursed down her face and disappeared as they fell. Her eyes were wells of sorrow. She had tried a second time to stay the Devil and had failed.

Thomas was staring at her, wide eyed.

The Devil gritted his teeth at her and twisted the door handle, nearly snapping it off in his haste. He stumbled from the car, nearly fell, and scrambled to the front and the door of 215.

White light was seeping from around the doorframe, seeming to drip and puddle at the base of it. He staggered, blood draining from his face. He hadn't seen that light in a very long time, the longest time, yet he remembered it…and he knew its purpose.

It was here for Kelly as she passed.

Fury ripped through him, seeming to peel the skin from his muscles, muscles from his bones, pouring liquid fire through his distending veins. A roar of outraged grief bellowed from his lungs.

Thomas, who'd been exiting the car, dropped to his knees in abject terror.

The frustrated knocker in 216 pissed his pants as his heart skipped jerkily in his chest.

The clerk, just about to tally out for the end of his shift, fell face-forward over the register as a blood vessel burst in his head with deadly result.

In room 215, Carrie turned to look at the door, her hands going slack on Kelly's throat. Terror whipped through her system but she misidentified the feeling as adrenalin. She grinned, not realizing her grin was a grimace of mortal fear—to herself, she was fearless. She strode to the door and yanked it open.

"OKAY MOTHERFUCKER YOU WANT TO GO LETS—"

She got the impression of something monstrous, with huge clawed hands and a bone encrusted head, hunched shoulders and rivers of burning blood flowing with a continuity that seemed endless as time itself. Then it was upon her, crashing into her like a freight train, tearing breath from her lungs. She was flat on her back, the beast over her. She looked up and into eyes burning with a fire that seemed somehow old, ancient, terrifying in its tenacity.

Finally, she knew fear. She blinked and the eyes were blue, the eyes of a man. His hands were going around her throat, and she knew fear. She blinked again and the eyes were burning pits and she didn't want to see…didn't want to see…she didn't deserve this–!

Then the weight of him was gone and she sat up, choking and coughing. Holding her throat, she turned to look at the bed.

The man/monster put his hand to the lace binding Kelly's hands and it crisped and fell away, leaving no mark upon her skin. Her hands fell lifelessly to the bed. The man/monster sat and gathered her body in his arms, holding her like a baby to his chest. He leaned over, crushing her to him. Enormous tears formed under the lashes of his closed eyes and poured like oil over his face and onto hers.

Black jealousy darkened Carrie's features.

"She deserved it," Carrie said, the words rasping out as she massaged her throat.

The man/monster on the bed paid her no heed. She coughed again.

"Fuck this," she said, and got shakily to her feet. "I'm out of here, bitches."

"Carrie." The voice came from behind her, somewhere in the vicinity of the bathroom. It echoed darkly against the tile.

Carrie's features drew down again. In confusion. In anger. In fear.

"Carrie," the voice said again. "Look what you did…you've saddened all of Heaven."

Carrie turned to look at the bed and her eyes widened in surprise. A handful of people, ghostly but there, ringed the bed. As she watched, more figures appeared, seeming to coalesce from the white light that floated across the floor like ground fog.

The figures seemed made of the white light, their features monotone yet distinct enough that she could make out every eyelash, every pore of their shining skin. They each gazed upon the man/monster and the body of Kelly with somber faces but there was something more in their faces, an emotion that Carrie couldn't identify.

"That's love," the voice said. Carrie turned sharply to the darkened bathroom doorway. "You don't feel that one."

A smirking gray cat sauntered from the shadowy bathroom. It sat and curled its tail around its forepaws.

"That's why you don't know it when you see it." The cat didn't open its mouth, but Carrie knew it was the cat that was talking; mocking her. She heard it in her mind.

"Fuck you, cat," she said, her voice low with warning.

The cat's tail twitched in amusement.

"Why don't you come over here and make me?" It said

into her mind and smirked again. "Scared of a little pussy?"

It winked.

Carrie threw herself at the cat and the she felt a shiver of alarm as the cat leaped toward her. The cat's head connected with hers and she suddenly had a sensation of fullness, of something rudely shoved in. It reminded her vaguely of sex and then she was falling, falling through herself, pushed down and down into the back of her own consciousness.

Sitri sat up in Carrie's body.

He grimaced at the smell and state of his clothing. He looked within to where the little hellion was trapped. Her tiny spark of consciousness was awash in lost despair. Sitri nodded his pleasure at her distress.

Then he turned to the bed.

The ghostly crowd still ringed the Devil and the girl. They moved like seaweed in a gentle current, almost like dancing as they started to fade. Sitri watched them dance and felt jealousy and love in equal measure. He'd not seen his kind in a very long time. He'd not been their kind for a very long time. Not since he'd followed Lucifer in his fall from Grace.

He looked between and through the Angels to locate the figures on the bed.

Lucifer still cradled Kelly's body. His face and hers

shone with his tears. He put his lips to hers and breathed out. His breath swirled hot and rich into her lungs and he placed his hand over her left breast. His hand warmed her even as the heat of life was leaving her body.

The fading Angels pushed forward and crowded before Lucifer, layering themselves one on the other like overlapping x-rays. Lucifer lifted his head, his eyes closed and breathed in, his mouth wide. The Angels floated into Lucifer and the Devil felt it again—what he hadn't felt since the Fall.

He felt what it was to be Divine.

He bent to Kelly again and breathed out, bathing her in radiance, in liquid Angel light.

Kelly's chest hitched and he felt the muffled thump of her heart under his hand. It thumped again as her breath left her.

She drew in another breath on her own.

Kelly opened her eyes.

The Devil was stunned all over by their deep emerald color, the glorious beauty they held, the Glory.

"Kelly," he whispered. He traced a shaking hand down the curve of her face. "Kelly, it's you. It was you all along." He saw the truth in it even as the words crossed his lips. Had it not been for his interference on this Earth, Kelly would most likely have been killed.

Had been killed, really, until the Angels helped him intervene.

Kelly nodded.

"God told me you would save me," she said and burst into tears of her own. They mingled with the Devil's tears already on her face.

The Devil turned and looked at Sitri, his eyes a question.

Sitri stood in Carrie's body and shrugged his shoulders, but his eyes had gone wide. Humans were not capable of hearing God's voice. Or so it had always been.

What made this woman, this human, different? Why had God put the Devil, Himself on the Earth to save her?

What was she meant to do?

Sitri shook his head but couldn't take his eyes from Kelly. Traces of the Angels presence seemed to glitter on and just above her. Each breath she took stirred the essence into cool, shimmering fireworks.

She was beautiful.

The Devil gathered her against him. He kissed each eye and each cheek. He kissed her forehead. He sat her up and held her as she steadied herself.

She put tentative fingers to her neck, to where Carrie's knife had drawn a thin line of blood and where Carrie's hands had squeezed and crushed. She turned to the Devil and lifted her chin.

"Is there a mark?" she asked, giving him her throat, vulnerable as a new lamb.

"No, no mark," he said. He saw that even the surgery scars from her youth had been lifted. Her skin was un-flawed.

She smiled at him.

He stood and put his hand out to her.

She saw past him to Carrie standing awkwardly at the end of the bed and alarm flashed into Kelly's eyes and then was gone. She would have recognized the real Carrie from horrifying experience. She nodded and Sitri, dressed in Carrie's body, nodded back.

Kelly stood and took the Devil's hand.

A gray cat lay in a heap by the door, its tongue hanging from its mouth. Sitri bent to it and put his hand on the cat's side to see if it still breathed. It did. Then it twitched, opened its eyes and sat up.

Sitri lifted it and stared into its face. The cat stared into his and then blinked. And then the cat blinked again, looking away. Just a cat, after all.

Sitri smiled and turned to Kelly.

"Want a cat?" he said and thrust the gray bundle toward her.

She reached out instinctively to keep the cat from tumbling to the ground. It put its paws over her shoulder and clung to her, head near her ear. She hugged it and a rough, out of practice purr started up in its chest.

The Devil opened the door, Kelly and Sitri behind him. It was much warmer and the sun hit him full force, blinding him momentarily. Then his eyes adjusted.

Kelly's car sat right where she'd left it.

Thomas Evigan, however, was gone.

* * *

Sitri and the Devil sat in Kelly's kitchen. The Devil had just looked in on her. She slept, untroubled. The gray cat lay on the bed between Kelly and the door, front paws tucked under his chest. But he did not sleep. It was as though he was keeping watch over his new mistress.

In the kitchen, the Devil let his eyes travel the length of Sitri. He still wore the pirate boots and ripped jeans, the vest and shrug. He had pulled his mass of greasy hair back and tied it in a rough knot: it looked almost like dreadlocks. It suited him, really, although as Sitri passed a hand across his hair, the Devil could tell he was missing the pompadour he'd had with the stylish old man.

"You should have let Kelly give you some clothes. You look like a Patron in your rended garments."

Sitri laughed but the Devil merely smiled and even that was quickly gone.

"I'm going to turn her in," Sitri said, smirking. "This time I can guarantee she'll go to prison. I know exactly where the bodies are buried, so to speak, and of course I will confess to everything. Can you see me in women's prison? It will be glorious! And she will suffer the whole time." He looked at his own midsection, his voice rising as though he addressed a deaf person. "Hear that, darling? We'll have years and years together, you and I!" He grinned and then leaned forward and sipped from a mug, and then he grimaced. "This is terrible," he said, swirling the dark contents. Coffee grounds floated into view and out. "Why do they drink this? Self flagellation?"

The ghost of a smile flitted over the Devil's features again and was gone just as quickly as the first time.

"How will I find him now, Sitri?" the Devil spoke into his own mug. His voice was low, despairing.

Sitri shook his head.

"I don't know, Lucifer," he said. "If I were him, I'd be as far away as I could get. How much time do you think you have left?"

The Devil consulted his instincts, trying to see. "I don't know, but not much I don't think. Not enough to start all over." He shook his head. "Now he'll have a long, fulfilling life. The unfairness of it just…" he shook his head again, once left, once right and sat back in his chair, pushing the mug away. "But no matter. It is His will."

Sitri nodded and sighed, "His will be done."

There was a knock on Kelly's front door.

Sitri and the Devil looked at each other, Sitri's eyebrows raised.

The Devil shrugged and stood.

He went to the door.

* * *

When Thomas Evigan had recovered himself in the parking lot at the motel, he'd gained his feet and crept to the door of room 215. He put his eye to the crack but could see very little at first—it was very dark inside. Thomas didn't, couldn't, see the Light or the Angels as they appeared one by one.

His eyes just didn't work that way.

Carrie half lay, half sat on the floor, coughing and massaging her neck. Thomas followed the direction of her gaze. He saw the Devil on the bed cradling Kelly's body. It was obvious that she was dead. That's when it finally occurred to him to wonder what he'd put up in the bargain. What it was he now stood to lose. He became very afraid.

His attention turned to Carrie when she said: "She deserved it."

Then: "Fuck this. I'm out of here, bitches."

And then, very oddly: "Fuck you, cat."

She'd turned away, facing the bathroom where the

Devil's cat sat staring at her. Thomas felt a surge of distaste at seeing the cat. Then Carrie and the cat leaped at each other.

From Thomas' perspective, he saw the back of Carrie and the front of the cat. Its yellow eyes were glowing like lamps as it charged and then Thomas saw what he would remember for the rest of his life:

He saw something on the verge of emergence, something fiery and horrific. It was a demon's face shimmering like a transparent mask just above the cat's features. Carrie and the cat connected and for a brief instant, Thomas saw the entire demon, somehow snake-like, rat-like, crow-like suspended in mid-air. It was grinning furiously, hands/paws/claws extended, excitement lighting its features…then it disappeared.

Into Carrie.

Thomas had never seen anything more horrifying in his whole life.

He fled.

He ran first to the motel office, his mind overwhelmed by a panicked litany: the police the police will help I'm a taxpayer the police will help they have to I pay taxes they work for me–

A fat, dirty clerk was lying across the counter, blood dribbling from his nose. His eyes stared sightlessly at Thomas.

Now his mind picked up a new litany: the devil did that the devil killed him it was the devil the devil oh christ now what…

He backed out of the office and ran back to his car, digging in his pockets for his phone and keys. He couldn't find either. He slapped all his pockets and slapped them again. He remembered the phone was in his jacket pocket at work. He remembered that the keys were in the ignition.

He slid behind the wheel, panting, his scalp tight and his sphincter even tighter. He keyed the engine to life and backed in a large semi-circle, getting the car nose-out to the highway. He saw a break in traffic and as he pulled out, he glanced in his rear view mirror.

The door to 215 was opening.

The Devil walked out, looking back, holding the door for someone behind him.

Kelly walked through the door.

She was smiling.

She was beautiful.

Thomas shot out into traffic.

He drove eight panicked miles before calming slightly and pulling over for gas. While the attendant filled his tank his mind began to work the bits of information he had, categorizing, arranging, analyzing and discarding.

Kelly was not dead. That was the most important piece

of the puzzle right now: Kelly was not dead. Briefly his mind tried to sidetrack as he recalled how beautiful she'd looked...Kelly had never been beautiful or even pretty. She was a plain woman. He knew that, but now...how had that happened? He shook his head. That didn't matter, his mind told him with calm authority, it only matters that she is alive.

Without you, she'd be dead.

You saved her life.

It was true, he decided, he had saved her life. Pride grew within him. He was a hero. A savior. He deserved everything the Devil had promised him, and more.

He drove to his office first. He had some files he wanted to shred and some more he wanted to delete from his hard drive. When he became President, he'd be scrutinized very closely. He also needed to flush his coke. He'd get something better, something prescription, once he was the President. He'd never be denied anything, ever again.

He was riffling through old files, pulling them out and stacking them on the floor next to him, looking for one case in particular: it was one he'd really screwed the pooch on. He laughed, remembering. He'd missed a key piece of evidence and his client had—

The Carrie Walsh folder was at the top of the hastily stacked files. It popped open, seemingly of its own accord, and two photographs slid out and seesawed to the floor landing one on the other. They were both face down.

Thomas froze, his frantic searching coming to an abrupt halt. He stared at the blank backs of the two pictures, his blood running cold. He reached out and grasped them by their corners and turned them over. He looked like a poker player scrutinizing the two cards that would make or break him in the game.

The one on top was the photo of baby Brian alive, in a friendly dinosaur tank top. He was caught mid-stride, toddling toward the camera, one pudgy baby arm reaching for the photographer. His smile was wide and gap-toothed. His blond hair bounced joyously on his cowlick.

In his mind, Thomas heard ghostly laughter, a baby's happy giggle pulled through time.

The photo beneath was smaller and the edges were rough. It was one of the coroner's photos, taken right before they began the autopsy. The only recognizable things were the fluff of blond hair and the dinosaur tank-top—the rest of Brian was a broken, bloody ruin.

Thomas ran them through the shredder, shuddering. He turned away as they were chewed down into the machine. He heard another ripple of laughter but just before it faded away, it dissolved into tears.

He leaned on his desk, catching his breath. His heart

felt as though it were dragging through his chest, deflated and heavy. He couldn't get enough air in his lungs. The thought that had occurred to him the day that Carrie was acquitted occurred to him again: he had offended.

He had offended.

Stop it, his mind commanded. You're a hero. You're a savior. You've nothing to feel remorseful over. You did everything you had to do. Everything. And it's all going to come to fruition. All you have to do is go and get it.

He straightened and absently brushed away the tears that had slid, unnoticed, down his face. Hot in here, he thought distractedly, I'm sweating like a pig. Gotta get that air checked out.

Then he remembered that he didn't have to get the air or anything else checked out. He was going to be President. He was going to be rich with a beautiful, stupid wife, he was going to be handsome forever, he would never age...

Yes, his mind told him, it's time to claim your prize.

He finished in his office and then drove to Kelly's house. He assumed the Devil would be where Kelly was. He didn't admit to himself that he also wanted another glimpse of her...of her mysterious new beauty.

It occurred to him that he could tell her how he'd saved her life. He could woo her with the info. She was bound to be grateful. She was maybe too smart to be his wife, but she could be his mistress, he decided.

He'd forgotten completely that he'd been the one to put her in danger in the first place.

He parked his car in the street and sauntered to her door, his spirits lifting as he considered everything he would soon have. I'll have everything I deserve, he thought, and no less.

He knocked on the door.

* * *

The Devil opened the door to find Thomas Evigan standing on the small porch. Thomas' grin was wide: idiotically so. His eyes sparkled with chilly pinpricks of light: he had snorted a bit of his coke before flushing the rest of it down the toilet.

The Devil controlled his features, just barely able to keep his mouth from gaping open. He tilted his head and closed his eyes briefly.

"Thank you," he said, almost whispering, reverential with gratitude. He felt a weight lift away and float off into the clear afternoon sky. He smiled.

"You're welcome!" Thomas rejoined jauntily, stepping past him and into the house. He gazed around with fevered interest. He'd never given any thought to Kelly before, much less to how she lived. "Nice. Small, but nice," he said, tossing the words carelessly.

Thomas turned back to the Devil but his eyes skated over him and away. He took a breath.

"So, anyway," Thomas said and he sidled past the Devil toward the kitchen, his curiosity a wild thing in him fueled by the coke. "How do we work this? Will I be President all at once? Or do you, like, fix the elections or something?"

He turned into the kitchen doorway and beheld Carrie, sitting at the table, a cup of coffee before her. Carrie blinked at him in shock. Then a large grin overtook her face.

"Thomas!" she said. "I am very surprised to see you here!" She laughed.

Thomas began to smile, happy to see a familiar face.

"I could say the same! I mean…" his smile faded as he looked over his shoulder at the Devil who'd moved into the kitchen doorway. The Devil stood silent, arms crossed on his chest. Thomas turned back to Carrie. "You…you tried to kill Kelly. Why are you…" he turned back to the Devil. "Why is she here?" he demanded. He was suddenly afraid that she had also made some deal with the Devil. Perhaps one that would interfere with his own. "She tried to kill Kelly, I saved Kelly, don't forget that. Don't forget our deal!"

Still Carrie laughed, infuriating Thomas and now he

stood three feet from the Devil staring a shaky challenge into his eyes. The Devil only smiled.

"Don't worry," the Devil said, laying one hot and heavy hand on Thomas' shoulder. "That's not actually Carrie. Carrie is finally getting what she deserves. And more besides."

Thomas looked at Carrie, suspicion dragging his features together. Carrie grinned and mouthed something to him. It looked like 'meow'. Crazy bitch. Thomas' reply to her was a vicious sneer.

"Whatever, let's get the show on the road here." Thomas shook off the Devil's hand and pulled out a chair. He sat, his legs a wide v, arms crossed over his chest. He glanced at Carrie, at her insolent grin, and felt a distinct ripple of unease whose source he couldn't identify. Go figure, he thought sarcastically, that crazy bitch is making me feel crazy.

He turned his gaze back to the Devil and raised his eyebrows. It occurred to his coke-addled mind that for being the Devil, this guy was kind of a pussy. He laughed.

Then the Devil stepped toward him and Thomas' laugh was cut off as if on a switch. Another ripple of unease, stronger, poured through him.

He scrambled to sit straighter in his chair.

"Hold on now…we had a deal, remember?"

The Devil inclined his head slightly. Then he pulled out

a chair and turned it around, the back toward Thomas and he sat, straddling it. Facing Thomas.

"Please continue," the Devil said.

Thomas swallowed and tried to relax. This place was getting hot. Felt hotter in here than it had outside. Maybe the stove was on.

He tried to gather his thoughts before they could go galloping off in different directions. He found he was too flustered. He decided to cut directly to the chase.

"I want it all, everything you promised me," he said, finally.

The Devil smiled again, it played over his lips tugging first one corner of his mouth up and then the other. Then he laughed. Then he shook his head, once left, once right.

"No," the Devil said. He was still smiling.

Carrie laughed.

Thomas' head rocked back on his neck. He stared at the Devil with growing incredulity, but a part of him, the deep brain, the caveman, cried out for him to say fine, fine! accept it and leave before something terrible could happen.

Thomas heard that weak and mewling part of himself and quashed it once and for all. He stood abruptly and his chair clattered to the kitchen floor. He leaned over the Devil, his face was going red with adrenalin. Anger and fear smashed around inside him like colliding protons exciting his already volatile insides.

"You'll do it!" he yelled. He'd intended for his voice to come out deep and strong, authoritative, but it was reedy and thin instead. He continued on anyway, his face growing redder. "You'll give me everything I asked for: the Presidency, the wife, the money; all of it! You hear me! ALL OF IT! ALL OF IT!"

He stamped a foot for emphasis on both 'all's. He put his hands out to grab the Devil by the shoulders, to shake him into agreement, but in the end, found he couldn't do it. The cowering caveman part of his brain was too strong and his hands merely hovered in the air and then snapped back as he crossed his arms again.

"Well?" Thomas demanded, feeling jittery adrenalin whipping dizzily through his system, setting his nerves on hair-trigger alertness.

The Devil shook his head, once left, once right…and smiled.

Now Thomas' rage overflowed its banks washing reason and sanity away. He grabbed the Devil on either side of his face, his fingers digging in behind his jaw. He thrust his face into the Devil's.

"YOU PROMISED ME YOU PROMISED YOU BASTARD YOU PROMISED ME—"

His voice was cut off as the Devil stood and Thomas saw the fire that was kindling in his eyes. Black fire, red fire, black smoke, and souls…oh, the suffering of those souls…

He tried to pull his hands away from the fuming, grinning, burning face and found that he could not. His hands were welded in place. The Devil leaned in and now Thomas felt the heat from his eyes–from his entire body– and it seemed he felt himself warm in a solid sheet from forehead to toes.

It was like standing too close to a bonfire suddenly doused with accelerant.

"Thomas," the Devil whispered in his ear, and now Thomas felt the heat on that side of his face, felt the small hairs singe and he smelled the burning…his hair was beginning to burn where the Devil's face brushed against it. "I lied."

Thomas began to shake, teeth gritted, his eyes wide and dry. He felt his fingertips begin to burn, his toes and his ankles and the pain whipped into him and he could not move. He tried to close his eyes but they had dried open, his eyeballs beginning to bubble and he felt the agonizing growth of each small blister. His upper thighs and crotch heated up until it seemed a blowtorch had been turned on them. Finally his organs, the rich and meaty center of him, were bubbling like a stew. He opened his mouth to scream and his throat crisped at the first inrush of air and then the Devil's face was before him.

"You'll not have the life you desired for yourself; it offends me and is an affront to all mankind." The Devil's voice was low but Thomas heard every word, even though his ears had melted back into his head. "I will set you among the rest: the murderers and liars and thieves and you will burn for your sins and that burning will not end until God, Himself decrees it."

Thomas' clothes began to smoke and then fine curls of flame licked along the seams, blue and eager. The skin under his clothing first fused to the fibers and then his skin, too, was burning. He burned inside and out and his mind wanted him to faint, to die, but still he stood, shaking and aware.

There was no end to this burning.

No end to this torment.

He finally understood.

But it was too late.

"This is My Judgment," the Devil said, and Thomas burst into a pillar of flame.

* * *

The Devil stood at Kelly's bedside, Sitri next to him. The kitchen they had so recently deserted was clean and shining white–no trace of the raging inferno that had consumed Thomas Evigan and shepherded him to Hell.

The Devil gazed at Kelly's sleeping face, drawing comfort from the sweet calm he found there. An early evening breeze blew the curtains and they fluttered into and through the Devil but he didn't notice.

He was fading.

"Tell her…" he whispered. "Tell her that…" He shook his head.

Sitri waited patiently. He knew what it meant to Transition. He did not envy Lucifer the journey.

"Tell her that she makes it bearable," the Devil said, his voice breaking over the last word.

Sitri nodded as a tear slipped from his eye. He wiped it away.

"What do you think she's meant to do?" Sitri asked.

The Devil shook his head and faded a bit more.

"God only knows," he said. He wouldn't take his eyes from Kelly.

Sitri smiled and wiped another tear from his cheek. He turned and started from the room but paused in the doorway, his back to the Devil.

"I have to get going. I'm taking this body to the police and turning it in."

The Devil glanced at his friend.

"How long will you stay in it, Sitri?"

Sitri turned and grinned.

"In women's prison? As long as it's fun, my friend. As

long as it's fun." He winked.

The Devil summoned the ghost of a smile and then turned back to Kelly. He was almost completely transparent, now. Sitri stared for a moment longer, his features falling into sorrow, and then he turned back out the doorway.

"See you soon, Lucifer," he said, his voice a whisper, and disappeared down the hall.

The Devil leaned close to Kelly's face, studying her features. He wondered briefly the same thing Sitri had asked: what is she meant to do? And then the question dropped from his mind. He found he didn't care; he only cared that she was still in the world. Her presence alone eased the burden of The Litany, even if it meant she kept just one other person from joining it.

He stood straight again. He could feel the cold creeping over him, the despairing and lonely time of the Transition. But he could bear it. And he could bear his role in Hell. Until God, Himself made His own final Judgment.

He reached one faint hand out and laid it over hers.

"Love you, Kelly," he thought, and was gone.

* * *

In Philadelphia, a woman exiting the movie theater screamed as a body appeared on the sidewalk before her.

Her husband, who'd stooped to tie his shoe, did not see the body appear, but he looked up in shock at his wife's scream. Then he saw the situation and calmed. He stood and put an arm around his wife's shoulder.

"It's okay, hon, relax. I'll call the cops," he said and keyed his phone to life.

"You…you didn't see…?" she asked, her hands twisting against themselves at the level of her breasts.

"Yes, I see him, honey, what's wrong with–hello? Yes, I need to report a body…"

His wife fainted.

* * *

In Kelly's bedroom the phone rang. She struggled up to her elbow, feeling groggy and confused, unaware of what woke her. A sudden gust of wind blew her curtains in, and thunder rumbled somewhere close by. The setting sun struggled past the gathering storm clouds and everything seemed licked by its orange fire. She'd slept the day away.

The phone rang again.

Kelly picked it up.

"Hello?" she said.

"Ma'am, my name is Sergeant Angela Ortiz and I'm calling from the Philadelphia Police Department? Are you Ms. Kelly Anders?"

Static erupted on the line as lightning struck somewhere between her and Philadelphia.

"Yes," Kelly said, her voice faint. She strained to hear voices from the kitchen, hoping for the rumble of two demons passing the time, but she heard nothing. Her house was as still and silent as it had ever been.

"Ma'am, I'm afraid I have some bad news…it's about your brother…"

Thunder rumbled again and then the Heavens opened. Rain poured down as if thrown from buckets and Kelly had a flash of memory from childhood: one of her friends telling her that every time you committed a sin, the Angels cried. That was what made the rain.

She sat up and faced the window, the phone dropping from her hand. Sergeant Ortiz's voice became far away, shot through with static.

Rain blew in, spattering warmly across her cheeks, like tears.

Kelly joined the Angels in their sorrow.

.

BOOK SIX

The Devil's Gift

The Litany snapped and twisted its bilious horrors through the Devil's consciousness as ever it had done…the thieves and murderers, torturers and liars all made themselves known from their places on Earth as they went about the trivial, empty lives they led and that would amount to nothing, in the end.

When they passed on from their useless existences, they tumbled into Hell, where the Devil knew to expect them. He rolled out the red carpet of Hell's fire and punished them all, never with judgment, never favoring one over the other; he punished all equally. He blew great gouts of flame from his own running blood, burning and burning the damned who were without the hope of clemency, because none had ever sought clemency in honesty nor in their hearts.

It was as God, Himself, decreed it should be. And so it was.

Since his return to Hell, a new strain ran through The Litany and it was a shining thread of purest white. It coursed smoothly even as the others twined and twisted amongst each other like a frenzy of snakes bent on destruction. Its presence alone calmed the Devil's sleep and eased the burden of The Litany on his waking mind.

This, too, was as God, Himself, decreed it.

The Devil knew that this thread, this cooling string of information that flowed so easily within and without The Litany, was God's gift to him; it was the Devil's reward.

And what was his reward?

It was Kelly's life.

Kelly's life hummed past, calm and content, singular and without complication—the antithesis to the bulk of The Litany. He was aware of her, year by human year, and his love hummed along with her even if it was only a tune he hummed to himself.

How fast is our time on Earth compared to the time-less burning in Hell, the endless conflagration that all sinners will suffer until the end of this world. How quickly our lives must fly by in the Devil's consciousness, as he stays bent to the work that is his own punishment for the sins he has committed. Sins for which atonement may some day be granted, because the Devil, Himself, does ask for clemency and he does so from the depths of his honest heart.

However quickly it came and went, the Devil knew that Kelly's shining thread would sustain him miracu-lously even beyond the reach of its grasp...and he was able to content himself with it.

It was as He decreed it.

Christine Dougherty

EPILOGUE

Rosie drove with one hand tight to the steering wheel and cupped her midsection protectively with the other. Snow fell so thickly that the tracks of her tires faded to ghostly nothingness within moments of her passage. Her headlights illuminated the swirl of bright white flakes that hung like a dense lace curtain in front of her car.

It was the worst storm the East Coast had ever seen and Rosie drove through it in labor.

Joey was supposed to be with her, but he'd gotten stuck at the hospital; he was a nurse and because of the sudden storm, his entire shift was being held over. During their frantic exchange on the phone, he'd offered to come to her apartment to pick her up, but it would have been forty minutes to get to her and then back to the hospital. She told him she'd meet him at the hospital instead. She was barely having contractions and would have herself there in twenty minutes anyway; no problem.

Now she wished she had him here with her. Her twenty-minute drive had already lasted fifty and she wasn't even certain how much farther she had to go. She couldn't see anything.

Joey had become very dear to her in a short space of time. They'd met at the hospital when she'd come to visit a girl she worked with, Sandy, who had pneumonia. Rosie had just found out that morning that she was nine weeks pregnant. She couldn't believe she'd been so dense as to not notice the changes in her body but she supposed she hadn't really wanted to know.

She'd been sitting in the waiting room after a nurse had shooed her from Sandy's room to adjust something with her tubes. Rosie stared blankly at the light green wall and then all at once, she'd been crying. Sobbing, actually.

The nurse poked his head into the waiting room.

"All clear, you can go—" He'd been next to her in a second, patting her back. "She's gonna be okay. I know…all the tubes and stuff…scary, right? But honestly…she's fine. You've got nothing to worry about!"

Rosie looked up, hitching in a breath and he'd smiled and grabbed a box of tissues from the end table and sat next to her.

"Here you go. Clean up." He smiled again, his mild brown eyes warm and friendly. "Feel better? Sometimes you feel better after you cry…chemicals or something. I read that somewhere."

She nodded, blowing her nose.

"I read that, too." Her voice was shaky with exhausted tears. "Makes you wonder about people who never cry. Are they just jam-packed with those crappy chemicals or what?"

"Gosh, I don't know, I never thought about that part of it."

He said and tilted his head thoughtfully. "Are you and Sandy best friends? She really is going to be okay, you know. I wouldn't lie to you about that." He placed his right hand unconsciously over his heart and she fell for him a little bit, even though she already knew he'd never fall for her. Girls weren't his type, she surmised. "I'm Joey, by the way, Joey Antoinella."

"I'm Rosie and it's nice to meet you, Joey, but I'm afraid I'm not crying about Sandy…I mean, I feel terrible for her…but, I'm really crying for myself." She smiled and more tears lined up to take their suicide slide, but she sniffed them back. "That's really rotten, isn't it?"

He ignored her last question entirely.

"What's wrong?" He looked at her with such heartfelt concern that–even though she hadn't intended to–she told him about being pregnant. The concern never left his face; it was obvious that it was something she wasn't happy about.

He took her to the hospital cafeteria and they sat over cups of coffee and she told him her story. She had no idea at the time that coffee with Joey would become a weekly ritual, and one that she looked forward to more than she looked forward to anything else in her life, lately. He was just so comforting.

She told him about being new to the area, no family or real friends; even Sandy was just someone she knew from work. The only reason she'd been the one at the hospital that day was because she'd been elected to drop off the card and flowers that were from everyone in the factory.

"Joey, I'm only nineteen and my job is…" She laughed and shook her head. "I mean, it's barely a job, you know? It barely pays for anything. How can I afford this baby?"

He'd offered options: go home to her family (she had none, really, just an aunt somewhere who she didn't even know), contact the father for money (she'd balked at this; wouldn't talk about the father at all), and finally he'd offered for her to come live with him.

Rosie had been surprised, but not completely surprised. She and Joey got along so well right from the start, that, if she believed in such things, she'd have said they knew each other in a past life.

He said maybe she could go back to school, start with some online courses; he'd help with the baby.

"You know," he said, "I have three little brothers and two little sisters…I'm really good with babies!"

For Rosie, Joey was the best thing that could have happened to her. He was, quite literally, the answer to her prayers. So it had been decided that Rosie would move in with Joey once the baby came. It even coincided pretty well with the end of the lease at her current apartment.

She'd felt extremely lucky and in the last three months of her pregnancy, had even come to anticipate it with cautious happiness.

Now, squinting into the storm, trying to see beyond the lace patchwork of falling snow, she rubbed her stomach, reassuring the baby, reassuring herself. Everything would be fine; she'd be at the hospital any minute now. No problem. No worries.

She felt the nose of her car dip and a flutter of panic stirred in her and then the car was nose down, accelerating, falling into the storm. She slammed her feet onto the brake, but could get no purchase as her car bumped roughly down a snowy embankment. She realized what was happening seconds too late. She'd driven right off the road.

The gully at the bottom of the embankment was full of water and her car cracked through two inches of ice and slid down, slowing, sinking, the water coming to just above the bottom of the door before it finally stopped.

The car stalled out.

With shaking hands, Rosie tried to start the engine. The tired and helpless rrrr rrrr rrrr told her it was not going to start, but she keyed it and keyed it again, her breath pulling into her chest in panicked gasps as she sobbed in frustration.

She abruptly let go of the key and sat back. Her hands went around her stomach. It calmed her instantly.

"It's okay, baby, I'm going to get us out of here," she said, her voice a whisper. "It's okay, sweetie, I've got you, mamma's here." It was the first time she'd referred to herself that way and it steadied her even more.

She struggled her door open but it wouldn't go far; it was held in place by the ice on the pond. She pushed harder, grunting, and felt it give a little. She turned in the seat as well as she could and pushed again with all the force as she could muster. The door swung open as the ice cracked apart and she felt a surge of joy. It was quickly shunted aside as she felt hot wetness flood her thighs and bottom…peed myself? she thought, but then realized: her water just broke.

A contraction of stunning intensity hardened her middle and she cried out, bending over herself as much as the steering wheel would allow. An overwhelming need to push came over her but she knew she mustn't. The baby can't come now. It just can't.

As if in defiance of her panicked thoughts, another contraction hit, making her feel as though her entire midsection had suddenly become somehow more affected by gravity. Everything felt pulled down; the pressure was breathtaking.

She struggled to turn, to get her feet out the door. She dipped them down into the icy water and it felt as though her feet and ankles were burning and then they quickly numbed. She struggled forward, keeping the car on her left, going toward the rear of it. She couldn't see beyond her own outstretched arm, the snow was too heavy, but she knew the embankment was behind her somewhere.

She just had to get back up it.

She was as far as the trunk and clear of the water when another contraction hit, bending her almost double. She went to her knees, groaning, the snow soft as a blanket below her. She longed to lie down in its fluffy softness; it would cool the fever that seemed to have gripped up her insides. But she knew she couldn't. If she laid down, she'd never get back up. She couldn't do that to the baby.

She pushed herself up, panting.

"I'll make a deal with you, okay baby?" She put one hand under her belly and the other hand out and she moved away from the car, her foot reaching the incline of the embankment. "You don't come right this second and I'll get us out of this." She huffed out a small chuckle. "Okay, sweetie? We got a deal?"

She'd been making her way shakily up the slope, one foot at a time, keeping one arm out, reaching for little handholds. The grass under the snow made it slippery as a ski slope. Her hand was numb. She couldn't judge how far she'd gone or how much farther she had to go. Snow pelted her face and she seemed to feel each flake as a burning, stinging piece of ice. She wanted to sit down. Another contraction hit and she felt a black wave of despair...she wasn't going to make it. She was too tired and the bank was too steep, too slippery.

She slid down, losing half of what she'd gained and the despair came again, even stronger than the contractions.

She looked at her feet and the snow had bloomed with a blood rose that looked black in the dark...the baby was coming.

I'm not going to make it, she thought, bewildered and shocked. What about the baby? God help me, I want to save this baby. A wave of faintness blurred her vision and she tilted dizzily backward, almost down the slope.

A hand found hers in the dark, gripping her wrist and then her elbow. Then the someone was beside her, an arm around her back, helping her stand, helping her up the embankment. Rosie tried to ask his or her name, but the wind and snow pulled her words from her mouth and threw them up into the night.

They reached the road. An SUV idled on the shoulder. Rosie could see the hulk of it behind its twin cones of headlights, but it was indistinct, almost ghostly in the storm. The flashers were on, strobing warm yellow light into the gloom and Rosie thought she'd never seen something so welcoming.

Another contraction overtook her and she stumbled again, and went to her knees. This time, she didn't think she'd be able to get up, but then the hands were in her armpits, pulling her up. Then they were around her chest, and the extra support was heavenly. Rosie sighed in gratitude.

They shuffled together to the rear passenger door of the SUV and it was opened. The hands helped her in and she sat gratefully on the wide back seat. Heat poured over her and she began to shake in compensation.

Rosie looked back at the door. A woman stood, smiling in at her. Her features were plain, but strong, like a face you'd see in a painting. Her eyes were extraordinarily beautiful.

"I'm Kelly," she said. "I'm going to take you to the hospital."

"I'm…I'm Rosie," Rosie said and her eyes slipped closed as tears coursed down her cheeks. When she opened them, the woman still stood smiling at her. "We…the baby and I…I don't know if we would have made it if you hadn't come along. How did you know I was down there?"

The woman's smile faltered and puzzlement fogged her emerald eyes.

"I'm not sure. I just had this feeling. It was the strangest…well…the second strangest thing that's ever happened to me." She laughed, but it was a private laugh, something Rosie knew she was not meant to understand. Then Kelly reached in and grasped Rosie's ankle and squeezed it.

"Let's get you to the hospital. I'm sure everyone is anxious for your baby to be born."

The End

Christine Dougherty lives in South Jersey with her husband, dog and two cats. Visit Christine online at: www.christinedoughertybooks.com

Made in the USA
Charleston, SC
08 May 2012